Dani
xo
René

AMONG **ASH** AND
EMBER

DANI RENÉ

BETA readers - Carmen Jenner, Allyson Sherwood, Cat Imbault
Editor - Anna Bishop, Creating Ink Editing
Proofreaders - Illuminate Author Services & Main Manuscripts
Cover Designer - Jay Aheer (Simply Defined Art)

This journey was deeply personal, and writing Ash, Ember, and Kat's story hit me hard.
This book means so much to me, and I hope you enjoy the rollercoaster you're about to venture on.

No matter how broken you may feel, someone will see the light in between your shards and put you back together.

Dedication

To Cat,

Ash and Ember will always be yours.
Thank you for your love, support, and friendship.

Mad love,
Dani xo

PLAYLIST

Without Me - Halsey
Heaven in Hiding - Halsey
Lie - NF
Paralyzed - NF
Wonder if You Wonder - Witt Lowry
I fall Apart - Post Malone
Fading Away - Ollie
Drinking About You - Ryan Oakes
Breathe - Fluerie
War of Hearts - Ruelle
Hurts Like Hell - Fluerie
Miss You - Nathan Feuerstein
I Fell In Love With The Devil - Avril Lavigne
In My Blood - Shawn Mendes
Swan Song - Lana Del Rey
Always Remember Us This Way - Lady Gaga

For the full list, find me on Spotify

PROLOGUE
KATERINA

"YOUR PARENTS ARE DEAD."

The solemn words uttered by a deep voice ring in my ears like a foghorn in the darkness. Sounds meld into nothing. Only silence remains as I pull in a breath. It hurts to do it. My lungs feel as if pins are filling them.

When I exhale to keep the pain at bay, it doesn't help. The agony is so acute, it feels as if my chest has been sliced with a sharp blade and I'm left flayed before the two police officers who are watching me intently.

My gaze is locked on the armrest of the sofa across from me. Rather than on the police officer who's sitting on it. He'd introduced himself as Officer Dalton. The house suddenly feels cold. Not like the burning heat of my parents' store where nothing of them remains.

I lower my gaze to the gray sweatpants I'm wearing.

They're dotted with smudges of paint. I'd been working on a piece of art for the shop when the doorbell rang. The woman who was meant to babysit me while my parents were at work is still in the kitchen. I hear her clinking cups, or mugs, the sound of the crockery is so close it's as if she's right beside me.

"Ms. Nielsen," one of the men, Officer Lionel, calls to me, but I'm frozen in time.

My name is Katerina; that's what my teachers call me. Everyone calls me Kat.

But they don't know that. These men are not my friends. They're strangers.

My hands tingle as if I've been sitting on them for a long time, and I can't feel my fingers anymore. It feels like when winter bites at the tips, making them turn blue. My whole body shakes, trembling as if we've had a heavy snowfall and we're in the middle of a storm of epic proportions.

"Miss," Officer Dalton says, reaching for me, but I flinch the moment his fingers are on mine. Lifting my gaze, I meet a set of worried brown eyes, his hair is messy, it looks like he's been tugging at it. "Do you have any family to go to?"

I want to shake my head, but I can't move. My brain

has switched itself off, and nothing works. My limbs, my eyes, even my heart. It's stopped, and all I can do is sit there like a mute.

"Perhaps she's in shock. Let me get her some water." The brown-eyed officer leaves, and I want to shout at him, to scream and tell him not to go near my mother's kitchen because she likes to keep it neat and tidy. But no words come out. It's her space. The one place she ensures is perfect at all times, even when she's making her famous ravioli.

I don't want strangers to touch her things. It's bad enough the babysitter is fiddling around in there. They all need to leave. To go away and never come back.

Instead of shooing them out of the house, I just stare into nothing.

I don't know what I'm going to do. *A sixteen-year-old girl needs a guardian, but I'm grown up. I can be on my own. I mean, would the authorities allow me to live alone? Or do I have to find some long-lost family member to take me in until I turn eighteen?*

How do I say goodbye to my parents?
What do I do with all this stuff? Our home?
How am I going to get to school?
Am I going to graduate?

Do I take over my family's burned down store?

How do I say goodbye?

All these questions spill into my mind, turning over and over like a reel of black and white photos, which feels like it's never going to end. I suck in a breath, opening my mouth to tell the officer I want to be left alone, but no words come out.

They can't leave anyway. I know they can't. Once Mrs. Lowell goes home, I'll be alone, and I can't be alone. It's against the law for an underage child to be left without a guardian. But I'm not a child. I don't feel like a child right now.

I'm an orphan.

No family, no parents, and nothing but the pain that's sluicing through me.

If I had been at the store tonight, I could've helped them. Maybe I would've been able to save them, call for help. Guilt lances my chest over and over, and I find breathing difficult. I usually stay home when they're out working on orders.

A flower shop in the middle of the small town of Olive Grove, only two hours outside San Francisco. My father told me the beauty of living here is we get the best of both worlds—a city on our doorstep and the stillness of a town.

And now, the town has stolen them from me. I hate this place. This *forgotten, hidden gem* as it's usually called that took my parents and burned them to ash, leaving me with nothing.

Wetness drips onto my fingers that are twisted in my sweater. I glance down. Everything looks blurry, forcing me to blink. When I finally lift my hand and swipe at my face, I find it wet with tears. I'm crying, but I don't feel anything.

My focus is on the coffee table in the middle of the room. The glass top is lit by the reflection of the living room light. My mother would shine the surface every day, making sure there weren't any rings on the top, or any scrapes from my father's keys, which he used to dump on the table when he got home from work. He'd settle on the sofa and read while he waited for dinner.

"Here you go." Office Dalton appears from the kitchen; his heavy black boots don't make a sound on the soft carpet. He sets down the glass of water which is soaked in precipitation, and that's when it all hits me. They're no longer here. My mother can't shout at him for ruining her table. She can't even tell him to use a coaster.

As I pick up the glass, water spills over the sides. I

subconsciously draw my hand back behind me. Flinging the object against the living room wall, I hear it shatter. The sound drags me from my stupor, and I'm brought back to the painful present.

"Get out." My voice is raspy, but they hear me. They rise slowly, one of them stops before me like he wants to say something, and that's when I screech, "Get out! Get out! Get the fuck out!"

"If you need any—"

"I said, get out!" My voice is so loud, I wonder how I'm not shattering the windows in every room. Surely the neighbors can hear me.

Officer Dalton leans in closer, his face in mine causing me to shuffle backward. "I just want to let you know we'll give you some privacy. We can't leave yet, but we'll wait in the kitchen with Mrs. Lowell. Child Services will arrive to . . ." The words taper off into the silence, and he sets a card on the table, telling me to call them if I think of anything that could help the case.

Once I'm alone, my mind runs a million miles a second. More questions dawn on me then. *Will they find the person who did it? What would my parents want me to do? Will I be sent to a foster home? Is there anything left at the store? Do I bury their ashes?* There aren't any bodies left. They burned to nothing but piles of gray embers. And I wonder how one mistake can turn into an inferno. How can fire steal everything from me?

Once I'm alone, I sit back in my father's recliner, curling into a ball, I close my eyes, and that's when my feelings—all my emotions—spill free and I cry.

I sob like I've never done before. Until I can't breathe. Until my body is shaking so violently, my teeth chatter and my head throbs with a migraine. And I shiver while lying on the soft leather, unsure of what is going to happen to me.

I hear footfalls before I see the person enter the room. A suit—dark and foreboding—settles in the sofa opposite where I'm lying. I don't look at his face, but his voice washes deep calm over me.

"Ms. Nielsen, I'm here to talk to you about representing you in court," he says quietly. "I know you need time to think about everything that's happened, but I need you to contact me in the morning. I'm here to help you." He sits in silence, watching me, I can feel his eyes on me, but I don't meet his inquisitive gaze.

After long moments, he rises, sets a black rectangular card on the table on top of the officer's card, and leaves me alone.

I'm alone.

I'm all alone.

.

KATERINA

*T*WO *YEARS.*
Twenty-four months.
Countless days.
And far too many tears later.

I remember a time before this. My mother and father loved me. We were a family, and they tried to ensure I had everything. I remember the day I was told I would never be able to hear their voices again. The day I found out they were gone.

Details from that night are vague. My mind hasn't held onto much after the lawyer left his card. Child Services coming around; they told me I couldn't live alone. I didn't have any other family. I was a loner in a cold world.

They took me to an orphanage where I spent a month. I kept to myself, scared and unsure of how to go on without the people I loved. I wished for death to take me too. But he never came. All I'd ever wanted was to have a normal life—to go to school, study, and have a career that I loved.

None of that is possible now. It's so far out of reach, it hurts me every day.

I moved into a house with three other girls only a week ago. The room I'm renting is small with a single bed, a closet against the opposite wall, and a desk adjacent to it, that sits under the window which looks out over the city.

Even though it's not entirely run down, or dirty, I still miss home. My old bedroom was my sanctuary, and now I've got to make a new one.

Looking at my reflection in the mirror, and I don't recognize myself. I'm no longer a lanky teenager with Chucks and ripped jeans. Instead, a young woman with breasts and slight curves returns my stare. A young woman who may never get the chance to be normal because she is drowning in debt left to her by my parents.

Allowing the orange dress to drift over my frame, I twist and turn, taking in the elegant garment.

My new job demands perfection. Isobel—the girl who's helped me since I got out of the foster home I was placed in—has been a godsend. Even though I've never gone as far as some of the other girls in this house, I'm still what they call a companion—an escort. I'm the arm candy without benefits. That's one delicacy I've never willingly given to anyone.

When Isobel's boss added my photo to the website, she asked me if I'd like to use a pseudonym. I agreed, hoping to keep the *real* part of me hidden. Now, I go by the name Flame to the clients.

Katerina, the girl who could paint for hours, and play the piano to her heart's content is no longer here.

And I'm not sure how to get her back.

I haven't heard myself play in so long, I now doubt my ability to create music. The only songs I listen to are the emotional, heartbreaking rhymes and the melancholic rap of NF.

My earbuds blast the music so loud, it drowns out the whimpers and moans from the room next door. It's the only way I can forget what's happening only a wall away. They're not pained cries. Far from it. My flat mate is an exuberant beauty, who enjoys her job a little too much, and has clients addicted to her seductive personality. They visit daily, and it's never a surprise to see one of them coming and going from her room as if it were a five-star hotel.

Closing my eyes, I focus on the lyrics, on how the

rapper pronounces certain words. I listen to the pain so clear in his voice; it takes me to the place where I feel safe. It takes me to a home that no longer exists. I feel the burn behind the lids of my eyes, tears threatening as they always do. It's almost time to go out and find a client for the evening. And even though my heart is not in it, I know I have to.

Part of the job I've taken on is to be available every night. It's how I pay the bills for now. I wish I could find something better, but without a degree, and only my high school diploma, this is the only way to earn enough money to survive from day to day. Hopefully as I take on more clients, I can save for school.

I could work as a waitress, at the cinema, or even get a job as a cashier at one of the local stores, but it wouldn't pay me enough to survive, let alone save.

After our business burned to the ground, everything that I should have inherited—the house, the insurance pay-out from the store, and my college fund—were all gone. Swallowed up by debts owed to the bank. I didn't realize my father had been in trouble. I guess the boutique shop that he'd built from the ground up wasn't cutting it.

My mother, a stay-at-home mom, did the best she could, but not being able to work meant she'd had to rely on my father. I was the unaware daughter.

The lawyer explained there was still outstanding debt after the house had been repossessed. And once loans were settled, my college fund had been depleted.

Sighing, I head to my closet and look for the shoes I wanted to wear tonight. I'll be late if I don't get a move on. I'm lucky I am not under the stringent time guidelines the girls who work with me have. I merely smile and play nice until the evening is over, and the client and I part ways.

With Isobel's boss, Maria, offering to help find clients, I've been able to go on legitimate dates, rather than navigating my way alone, which could be dangerous. She's been welcoming, and I've allowed myself to trust her. Perhaps I shouldn't rely on someone so soon after meeting them, but she's given me references from previous escorts who worked for her which set my mind at ease.

Unlike the other girls, I work for myself and I don't have some pimp trying to steal my money. Maria allows me to keep all my earnings. The alternative would be giving someone else power over me, and that's not something I want to experience ever again.

A long time ago, after I was thrown in the orphanage, they put me into the system. I thought I'd be lucky. I was sent to a woman who was begging for a daughter to love.

Love was what she called it.

Abuse was what it truly was.

She was kind to me for a while, buying me pretty dresses, paying for my schooling with the money she received, but then she turned on me, and I had no way of getting out. The catalyst was when her boyfriend decided she wasn't who he wanted anymore, and she found him on top of me one night. She didn't believe me when I told her the truth—how he'd pinned me down. I recall the pain, the searing heat, and the agony that came with having someone steal a part of you that you could never get back.

Shaking my head, I open my eyes and push off the small single bed. The metal groans from the movement and I make my way to the closet. I pull it open, to find the right shoes which will go with the dress I bought at the secondhand store two days ago. It's not new, but it's pretty, and the color of burnt orange, reminding me of the glow of sunset on the horizon. Deep, vibrant, and intense.

Underneath I'll wear a black thong and bra to match. None of my clothes are new. The last time I got something from a boutique store was a lifetime ago when my father was playing his game of keeping up with the neighbors. To ensure everyone thought we were on the same level, he bought me everything I ever asked for. And it was all paid with credit.

After slipping down the pair of shorts I'm wearing, I step out of them and chuck them into the laundry basket. Perhaps tonight I'll make enough to go to the launderette tomorrow.

The dress is a silky material which slides over my slight curves. My tiny breasts don't offer much cleavage, but they will have to do.

At almost nineteen, I've been mistaken for a girl of sixteen. My springy brown curls hang down to the middle of my back, and I allow them to frame my face. My oval-shaped eyes no longer shine like they used to; now they're just a lackluster gray.

The thin straps of the dress hang over my shoulders, and the slight flare of the skirt allows my legs freedom, with the hemline sitting mid-thigh. It's pretty, and not overly sexy, but most of the men in the hotel I frequent know I'm not as seductive and experienced as Isobel. Or the other girls. Some of them are returning customers. Others just want to enjoy a good night out without their wives finding out. I don't care, as long as they pay.

"Flame!" Isobel's shout comes from the other side of my bedroom door. My only friend in this place must be ready to go. She knows her way around, and the thought of her accompanying me this evening sets my nerves at ease.

You'd think I wouldn't be nervous about meeting new people in my line of work. But every time I walk into the hotel bar and settle myself on a stool, it's there—the anticipation, anxiety, and the fear of not making it home that night.

"I'm coming," I call back, picking up the small silver purse she bought me as an early birthday present. I've given myself a goal to work toward. Twelve months. By the time I'm twenty, I'm hoping to move out of this place. My plan for college is on track. I just need a few more clients to sign up regularly, and I'll be able to pay half the scholarship for my first year of school.

Isobel wants to celebrate with me in a couple of weeks. She told me my birth should be a celebration, but all I really want to do is hang out in my room, drink cheap wine, and talk about the clients we meet that evening. Perhaps I'll be able to persuade her to change her mind.

Taking one last look in the mirror, I wonder if I'll ever be able to be Katerina again. Even though I'm determined to leave this place, I doubt I could ever be the carefree girl I once was.

I've learned how ugly the world can be.

And nothing can bring you back from those experiences.

When I finally step out of my bedroom, I find her standing on the landing with her hand on her hip. I offer her a nervous smile and follow her as we head down the stairs and out onto the road.

One day, it'll be the last time.

One day, I'll find myself again.

But until then, I have to work to live.

ASH

MY GAZE LIFTS THE MOMENT THEY WALK into the bar. Frederik Larson, one of my employees, sits opposite me. He's talking, but I don't hear what he's rambling about. My attention is on the two beauties who've just entered the lounge. They're both beautiful, but my eyes lock on the one in orange, the color of burning flint. The shade deep and rich, reminding me of the glow of embers, which makes me smile.

How fitting.

She sidles alongside her friend, perching her ass on a stool in the corner. Clever girl. From there, she can watch the room.

It's no secret as to what they're doing here. Not because they don't look like they belong in the hoity-toity crowd, but because I've seen her here before. I may not frequent the hotel, I only come here for the occasional meeting, but each time I've been over the past six months, I've seen her.

Mondays and Fridays.

On the other days, she's at another hotel. They're smart, meeting clients at different venues. I've known her boss for several years, and their comings and goings are the one thing I can certainly count on. Maria allows me to choose the girl I want in exchange for locations.

The beauty in orange glances around, taking in the room. My gaze is glued to her. Once she's focused on her friend again, she sips her drink, but I note how her eyes still roam the space. The corner of my mouth kicks into a smirk at the thought—beautiful *and* intriguing. That begs the question which has been plaguing me since the first time I saw her.

Why would a woman like her do what she does?

"And that's what we should be looking at, Mr. Addington," the old man tells me, catching my attention with the last bit of whatever he's just muttered about our plans for expansion. The company needs it, but before my father died, he was adamant about not allowing this asshole to run things. So in his will, he had a clause that my brother, Ember, and I would run Addington and Associates with Frederik Larson as an overseer.

Frederik can offer his opinion, but it's mine or my brother's signature that will seal the deal. Hence the reason Frederik's brought me here to buy my agreement with expensive whiskey and caviar, along with a woman for the night. Most of the board know about my proclivities, but they can't vote me out of running my father's company because my name is on the door. Father trusted me, and even though I've done some questionable things, I've never let it interfere with my work. The clause in his will states that if the company suffers, I will step down, allowing Ember to take over. So far, I've behaved. Somewhat.

I glance at Frederik who's going on about money and me allowing him to run the financial side of things alone. I know why he's asking because he wants to siphon what doesn't belong to him. The expensive looking box on the table is evidence that he's trying to buy my vote.

He doesn't realize that an Addington cannot be bought.

We do the buying.

We own the city.

I rise, then button my suit coat. Casting my glance toward him, I offer my hand and make sure he knows who's in charge. "Thank you, Fred. I'll be in touch."

"But—"

"Meeting's over," I tell him, knowing I need to play him at his own game. Also, there's a certain someone I'd like to own for the night. "We'll reconvene tomorrow in the office at eight." I turn and leave him spluttering at my back, but don't offer anything more.

When I reach the bar, I tap it twice, catching the barman's attention. He offers a nod, anticipating my drink before I even have to voice my order.

My gaze may be on the man mixing my drinks, but my attention is firmly locked on the woman I've asked Maria to send here for the night. The girl's lips quirk at her friend as she lifts a glass to her mouth, which captures my attention.

"Here you go, Mr. Addington." The barman grins as he sets my tumbler down.

"How about a bottle of champagne for the ladies in the corner," I tell him. It's not a question; it's a command. He nods, moving swiftly to grab one of the most expensive bottles and two crystal flutes, along with an ice bucket. I watch him work as he settles the bottle in the ice and heads their way.

A conversation I can't hear ensues, then he gestures with his head toward me. The girl in orange offers me a soft smile, shy, yet sensual. There's something intensely erotic about her. She's not at all like her overtly sexy friend. No, the girl I want is demure, and it makes my cock jolt with desire.

Her full lips move as she says her thank you, lifting the flute to her mouth and taking a sip of the bubbly liquid. Her eyes are wide, beautiful, and they hold secrets I'm tempted to unlock. I want to delve deeper into her mind and learn about the girl underneath. Surely she can do better than to whore herself out. When I noticed her on the website, even though I couldn't see her face clearly, I knew she had to be the one I'd been searching for. I was in disbelief at this beauty, attempting to put herself through school by selling her body.

Gulping down my drink, I head their way. As soon as I reach them, the giggling and whispering stop, and they both pin me with heated gazes. But I don't take notice of her friend; my eyes are on her.

"I trust you're enjoying the evening?" I question her, not even turning to look at the girl in the skimpiest dress I've ever seen. Her fake tits practically jump out as she leans toward me in an attempt to capture my attention.

"Thank you," the little flower whispers shyly. Once more, my zipper is starting to pain me as my cock throbs, begging to get a taste of the action. Aching to see just what lies beneath that silky material of her dress.

"Are you here for the night? Or...?"

"Uhm," she mumbles. "I'm . . . Well. . . if you're looking for company, I—"

"Yes," I interrupt her, offering her my hand. She gently slides her delicate one in mine, and I can't stop myself reveling at her smooth skin. "Let's get comfortable," I suggest. Tugging her along with me, I continue to ignore her friend.

I notice my beauty for the evening glance over her shoulder. Her mouth moves, but there's only silence, and I can't help but smirk. She's nervous. She should be.

I lead her to a small booth at the back of the bar area. From here, we can see everyone, but they can't see us. It's not my first go with one of the working girls in my city, but it's the first time I've dared to talk to her.

"I'm Flame," she murmurs shyly.

"Intriguing name." With a smile, I lean in to whisper in her ear. "What's underneath your dress, Flame?" The word on my lips drips with desire, and I notice her little shiver when my hot breath fans over her exposed skin. Goosebumps rise on her shoulder, making the smoothness disappear, and I'm tempted to trail my tongue along her collarbone to feel her shudder once more. So pretty, innocent, and far too sweet to be here.

Her fingers tremble when I suckle her earlobe into my mouth.

"Because you're not here for a few drinks with a friend. Are you?" I ask.

"I'm . . . here to work," Flame retorts heatedly, which makes my cock respond in kind, throbbing against my zipper again. "If you have a problem with it—"

Her words are cut off when I bite down on the lobe, scraping my teeth against the sensitive flesh, earning me a soft whimper. I know I have her right where I want her.

This pretty flower is no match for me.

I'm an expert.

A predator.

And she's merely my prey.

"Room nine three six," I tell her, sliding a keycard over the table toward her. When I lift my hand, I gesture with my chin toward the plastic object. "If you want work, I'll ensure you're paid very well. More than any man in this place can offer you."

Leaving her at the table, I head toward the bar, tipping my fingers to the barman in thanks before making my way to the elevators. The silver doors gleam with my reflection. Taking in my messy hair, I decide to get a haircut at some point. But then again, I love the just-fucked bed head look, so perhaps I'll take a page out of Ember's book and leave it as is.

When the elevator arrives, the doors slide open, spewing out a handful of guests and I step inside. Before I'm shut in the car alone, a slender body draped in orange slips through the small space between the closing doors.

"You accepted my offer."

"I need the money," she tells me honestly, shamelessly, and my respect for her has just been notched up by another two points. Life is a game, and if you don't play your cards right, you'll never win.

I don't look at her, keeping my focus on the red numbers that tell us which floor we're passing with every ding of the bell. "It takes courage to do what you're doing."

"More like desperation." Her voice grips me for a moment before I shake it off. That's one thing I never do: pity. Feeling sorry for someone doesn't give them confidence; it brings them to a point where they seek out sympathy, begging for a handout at every turn.

This girl, barely a woman, has probably been through more in her short life than I have in mine. And she's here, standing in an elevator with a stranger, ready to go into a hotel room to get fucked—all for a wad of cash to presumably pay her rent.

Or her boss.

That thought makes my blood boil.

Why? I have no idea.

"And does your pimp know you're in one of the city's most expensive hotels seeking your paycheck?" My voice is tight with frustration, jealousy, and anger, but she doesn't shy away from me. Instead, she sighs.

Flame turns to regard me with stormy eyes. "I work alone. This life"—she gestures to her ensemble—"is temporary. As soon as I can get out, I will."

I'm silent for a moment, pondering her words before I respond. "Like I said earlier—courage."

Before she can offer an answer, the doors slide open, and we walk onto the ninth floor.

I lead her with merely a touch to her lower back toward my room. The only suite in the hotel I ever stay in. When we reach the door, I slide the card into the slot and push it open. After ushering her inside, I shut us into the large space.

Leaning against the wooden entrance, I cross my arms in front of my chest and silently watch as she slowly makes her way deeper into the living room area. She doesn't look scared when she regards me again. Her eyes shine with anticipation. And I wonder if it's because I may be younger than her other clients, or perhaps she finds me attractive. I am certainly very fascinated by her. My cock is hard; it's ready to fuck her all the ways to Sunday, but I'm hungry to know more. Her mind intrigues me, and I'm dying to dip into the darkness.

I want to learn all about this princess who's taken a chance on a bastard like me.

KATERINA

HE STANDS THERE, LOOKING AT ME AS IF I'M THE most beautiful woman in the world. It's strange to have someone look at you, so different, to how you assume, everyone else sees you. It's as if he's staring right through me, seeing into my hidden depths, into those dark corners where all my secrets hide.

"You're trembling," he observes with a smile. There's a mischievousness to his expression, and I wonder just how old he is. Perhaps closer to my age than any other man I've been with.

He moves away from the door, and I watch as he saunters confidently toward me. Every step is calculated, and I have a feeling this man doesn't do anything just for the sake of it; he has a reason behind everything he does, from the way he shoves his hands into his pockets, to the way his head dips to the side as he regards me. Eyes the color of a cloudless sky watch me.

I'm not sure what to do with myself, so I fiddle with the strap of my bag. It's a nervous tick I've always had. My heart is thudding in my chest, attempting to break free and fall at my feet. It's the first time I've taken a man up on his offer of more than a date, and I'm unsure of what to do next. How does this work? I feel so inexperienced right now, it causes my cheeks to heat in embarrassment.

He's probably used to girls like Isobel. They know how to please a man. I've never been with anyone like this, not when I'm getting paid, and that thought makes my chest ache. This is my life now. If I want to make sure my bills are paid and finally get myself into school, I have to earn money. Big money.

Needing to keep my hands busy, I find my fingers twirled in the strap when he stops only inches from me. He's at least a few heads taller than me and about three times the size of me, and my heart leaps into my throat. Breathing becomes difficult as I struggle to find the air to pull into my lungs. His gaze is luminous as he regards me.

Can he tell I'm practically a virgin at this?

Am I merely a toy in his room?

Something he could use and discard?

His lips curl slowly as if he's enjoying my fear. The

29

pupils in his eyes dilate like he's a predator ready to pounce.

"I'm not scared of you," I tell him, my voice calm, steady, but I can't stop shaking. It's a lie, and I know he can see right through it. He tips his head to the side, observing me, making me feel like a piece of art he's thinking of purchasing.

Will he send me back downstairs now? Am I too innocent for him?

No. He asked for me. I mean, surely, he'll still pay for my time. Won't he?

My brain doesn't want to shut up. The noise is consuming as the silence in the room is heavy with tension. I want to speak, but words escape me around this handsome man. He is gorgeous. Far too breathtaking for me to handle.

He leans in closer, allowing his fingertips to trace a slow line down my shoulder, and his gaze follows their path. Finding my elbow, he grips it and tugs me closer to him, then lowers his hand once more.

Our bodies are flush, and I can feel his erection pressing against me, but he makes no move to touch me, or even kiss me. Nothing is separating us in this moment, and the heat of him is unbearable. I feel like I'm standing in the desert, about to melt from the merciless sun that's beating down on my flesh.

"Tell me who you are, Flame?"

His question stills me, causing me to furrow my brows. I don't do heart-to-hearts. This isn't a date, and he needs to know that.

"That's not how this works. We fuck, you pay, I leave." My voice cracks on the words because they're not my own. Isobel's mantra came easily to me. She's drummed it into my head for the past week.

He tips his head to the side at my confession, his eyes penetrating me like they're burrowing themselves right into my heart. He won't find much there, only ashes are left after the fire that burned my life away.

At my response, he doesn't refute me. Instead, his mouth finds the nape of my neck and his nose trails over the skin. I hear him inhale my scent. The motion is sensual, something I'm not used to, and I push away from him, forcing myself to meet his hungry, yet inquisitive, gaze.

He doesn't say anything, just tugs me along with him to the sofa. Once he's seated, he pulls me onto his lap, so I'm straddling his thighs. Our bodies fit together like broken pieces slipping beside each other to create a whole.

The hardness of him presses against my core. Only material separates us, and I wonder what he will feel like

31

without his clothes on. What he will look like naked.

"I'll fuck you," he promises with a wicked grin, and a dimple appears in his left cheek, spurring the butterflies in my stomach into a flurry of activity. His hands trail over my shoulders as his eyes follow their path. He watches me as his finger dip along my back, then over my hips and down to my legs. Silently, he spreads my thighs so wide it almost hurts and bunches my dress until he exposes my underwear. An appreciate groan rumbles in his chest when he notices the thong I'm wearing. His gaze is locked on his movements as he pushes it to the side and dips one finger into me. "You're already wet."

"I . . ."

"Does every client get you this wet?" he questions, and I wonder if it's a hint of jealousy I detect in his tone. I feel my cheeks heating at the realization that this stranger has me so turned on after only one touch. His hips rise, pressing me along the bulge in his slacks. Our connection is seamless—his hard edges fit along my soft curves.

"No."

"Are you lying?"

Shoving against him, I move to stand, but his hold on me is far too strong, and I can't get off his lap. His arm bands around my waist, keeping me right where he can touch me. His hand dips under my panties, and two fingers invade my entrance eliciting a whimper from my lips.

"I asked you a question, pretty girl," he says affectionately, causing my heart to flip-flop. My stupid, wild heart thuds against my ribs and they feel as if they're about to crack from the sheer force.

I lift my chin in defiance, hoping I sound stronger than I feel. "Like I said, we fuck, you pay, I—"

"I know what you fucking said, and like I told you, I'm paying for your time, and you need to obey me." He doesn't look like he's joking, his expression serious as his fingers find my core once again and he continues his ministrations. His thumb presses against my clit, circling it expertly, turning my body hot and needy.

He dips two digits into me, and my walls pulse around him. My hips roll, and he smirks below me. Those deep blue eyes look up, watching me as he works my body into a frenzy. I lose myself to the feeling, to the heat that's shooting through every nerve in my body.

I haven't ever done this before, but for some reason, all I can think about is my orgasm and giving it to this man. He crooks his fingers, rubbing a spot deep inside me, and the sounds coming from there make my cheeks burn with embarrassment as he toys with me.

My toes curl, my nails dig into the expensive material of his shirt, and I don't care if I rip it from his body because I want to see exactly what he looks like without the offending item of clothing. I want to lay him bare as he's done to me. The emotions that are catapulting through me cause me to whimper and moan.

I'm about to crest when he pulls his hand from me, causing a keening cry of frustration to fall from my lips. I open my eyes, meeting his satisfied grin. He's playing with me like I'm a goddamn instrument.

"This isn't what I do for fun, Mr. . . ." I utter as I glare at him for taking away the pleasure I felt only moments ago. I wait for him to tell me his name, to say anything, but I realize he isn't going to respond, so I continue, "This is my life. I've accepted it. If you're just here playing mind games with me, I'll go back to the bar and find another client who will pay up and get his rocks off so I can go home."

He doesn't miss a beat when he questions, "And where is home?"

"No personal—"

"This is my money, my time, and you're here to please me." He allows me off his lap, and I have to take a step back.

He doesn't rise, merely regards me from his seat on the sofa, looking like a dangerous, dark god—beautiful and deadly. His shirt is ruffled, his dark slacks hug his thighs, and his hair is messy.

His eyes narrow on me. He lifts his hand, resting his elbow on the armrest of the sofa, and he rubs his index finger along his chin. "So, little Flame, tell me where. The. Fuck. Is. Home?"

"Like I said—"

"Ten thousand," he interrupts me, silencing me with merely two words. He gives me a moment, perhaps to process what he's just said, but I'm sure he's lying. "Right now."

Tipping my head to the side, I open my mouth in shock before asking, "What?"

He's young, far too young to have that amount of money in his wallet. Then again, as I glance around the room he brought me to it's obvious he's wealthy. How can a man who doesn't look like he's even hit thirty afford a room like this?

"I'll pay you ten thousand for your time this evening. Just humor me." He smiles, reaching for me, pulling me closer toward him, so I'm once again perched on his lap. His grip is so tight, I can't move away. His hands stroke my thighs gently, as if it's normal for him having a random girl planted on his lap. The soft circles of his thumbs on my

35

skin make me tingle, and there's no way I can ignore his expert touch.

The movements of his fingers, along with the way he's watching me, ignite a fire deep in my gut. My nipples harden when his thumb swipes across my panties, pressing against the bundle of nerves that seem to ache for more.

"Tell me, sweet girl," he coos, low and seductive. "Where does this pretty little stranger come from?" His eyes blaze as a whimper tumbles freely from my lips. He nudges the material of my underwear aside and massages me like I'm the most delicate thing in the world.

His touch is commanding, yet affectionate, which heats my blood. My lips part, but I can't focus on the response. His thumb dips into me. It's not deep, not at all what I need, but the wetness gathers at my core as his expert ministrations make me tremble.

He pulls his hand from between us and places his thumb on his lips, then slowly licks the arousal from it. There's a fire in his eyes, a blazing desire, and I roll my hips, causing friction against his erection which is still prominent in his slacks.

"I live down the road from the hotel. Two blocks away," I whisper, breathing deeply, hoping he doesn't notice the inflection of need in my voice, but I know it's futile. This man can read me front to back like a book. Even if I wanted to hide who I am, where I live, or even the real part of me I've shoved so deep down inside, I don't think I could ever fool him. "What's your name?"

"I thought you said no personal details?" He chuckles when I glare at his question.

Shrugging, I allow my finger to trail down the buttons of his shirt. *Can I play the seductive kitten and undo them?* One by one, until he's exposed, allowing me to explore his torso, and I'm sure there are smooth dips and valleys where my fingers could roam. "Since you've been asking all the questions, I figure I should at least know your name?"

"Ash," he tells me with a slight nod. "And you're?" He waves his two fingers in the air, circling them as if offering me the opportunity to respond. "And not some street name you use; tell me your real name," he utters.

"I've never told anyone my real name. At least, not for a long while." My confession causes the sadness of losing the person I used to be grips me, but Ash's fingers tease my nipples casually, like it's natural for him to touch me anywhere he'd like.

He doesn't acknowledge me, but I know he heard me. He's thinking about his next move; I can imagine the wheels turning in his mind. Chess players take time to think about their moves, about how they're going to take their opponents down, and that's what Ash is doing. I haven't known him for long, but I can tell he doesn't just say something for the sake of it. "Tell me," he urges.

"Katerina," I utter my name. It's been so long since I've said it, the word feels foreign on my tongue. Like she's no longer me. I'm a guest in the body of the girl I used to know.

After two years, I am a stranger to myself. It's been a long while since I recognized the real me in the mirror. Each time I look, all I see is the stranger I've become.

"Katerina," Ash murmurs slowly and deliberately. It's like he's tasting my name on his tongue. He seems to like it because he smiles. "And you decided Flame is the name you'll use for this shit show?" He lifts his hand, once again gesturing to the air.

"I had no choice but to change who I was. I don't know why you care," I tell him before pushing on his chest. This time, he allows me to rise, and my dress falls over my thighs to cover my body from his gaze. "Not everyone has rich parents to pay their way." My words fall from my mouth before I have time to think about what I'm saying and the moment he hears me, I see the pain etched on his face. *Shit.*

"You think that's who I am?" he questions incredulously, I've just judged him for being in a fancy hotel, dressed in an expensive suit, and looking like a model who's just stepped off the runway. But then again, if he doesn't want to be seen a certain way, he shouldn't act the way he does.

"I call it like I see it," I respond, attempting to hide the guilt that's tightening my chest. Turning away from him, I head to the window, staring out at the city below. I wish I were somewhere exotic, but instead, my life has brought me to the streets of Seattle. I don't know if he lives in the city. If he does, the filth of the streets doesn't touch the penthouse or the hotel we're currently standing in.

We're safely locked away in a glass cage. Nothing can touch you when you're this far up. A prince in a cloud of safety—that's what Ash is.

"Do you have any siblings?" he questions from behind me. I half expected him to come to me, but he is still seated on the sofa.

I shake my head, fiddling with the material of my dress, remembering how lonely I was growing up. I never knew what it was like having a best friend. Not a sister or brother to fight with. And then, before I was old enough to realize it, I was completely alone.

"No. I was an only child." My response comes out angrier than I intend, and I know he notices it. There's something about Ash that assures me he's not someone who will disregard anything I say or take it lightly. I don't know if that's a good or bad thing, but I can't change how I feel, or stop expressing myself as I usually would.

"What's made you so angry, Kitten?" he asks, causing me to glance over my shoulder and take him in. There's a sadness in his gaze, but also so much curiosity.

"How old are you?" I blurt without overthinking it.

He laughs. It's the first real smile I've seen on his face, and I'm drunk on the way his expression lights up. His eyes crinkle at the sides, his mouth tilts, and his perfect white teeth peek at me. He is nothing short of flawless, which causes me to silently question what he's doing here, paying a girl for her company.

"I'm twenty-five. Almost twenty-six, actually."

"You have a birthday soon?"

He nods in response.

"When is it?" This time, I smile. It's the only day I've ever felt like the old me—on my birthday. When I was growing up, I used to have a big slice of chocolate cake and a mug of coffee while reading my book on the sofa. It was my ritual every year; my mother would bake, and we would have a slice for breakfast.

"No personal details," the man reminds me with a sly smirk.

I move toward him again, and settle myself on the sofa beside him, excitement lacing my tone as I ask, "Fuck that. Tell me?" I don't care about the way I curse outwardly. I forget who I am and where I am. And for a minute, I forget why I'm here. Right now, in this moment, I'm a girl, with a boy, and we're on a date.

"You're quite demanding." He turns toward me, giving me a playful wink. Ash relaxes his posture before responding, "It's in three weeks."

That's soon. Like, really soon. "Are you celebrating?"

"No, my brother and I just stay home. I might have a few drinks, but we don't party," he tells me, his tone turning serious.

All the fun that hovered around us is gone, and in its place is tension.

ASH

I'M NOT SURE WHAT THIS GIRL IS DOING TO ME. I brought her up here to get my dick wet, and now I'm confessing shit about who I am that I never tell anyone. It may only have been my birthday, but women who enter this room do not learn who Ashton Addington is.

They spread their legs, and get filled with my cock—not some fucked up story time about the Addington family lineage. But then again, Katerina doesn't know my full name or my family name. None of them do. It's anonymous. Nothing more than a one-night stand. Once I've found release, they leave.

"You don't celebrate?" she questions, breaking my train of thought and causing me to glance at her for a moment.

I want to tell her to leave. Mainly because I'm flummoxed by how intriguing she is, how she pulls information from me effortlessly.

Her dark wavy hair makes my fingers itch to tug it backward. I would love to hear her whimper. I fantasize about that sound falling from her lips. If I were to shove my cock down her throat, would she choke, or take me like a pro? Those beautiful eyes would surely be wide, shocked at my roughness, but I'm confused at how this woman can care more about my birthday than I do.

"No. My birthday is not something that should be celebrated." The words tumble from my mouth in a whoosh. If I allow my thoughts to continue, she will soon be on her knees. I want that, but I also want to talk.

Who knew a pretty little thing like her could make Ashton Addington want to have a conversation?

She frowns, rising from the sofa before she moves to the desk. Her body is beautiful. I bet she'd look good naked, lying on the mattress and open and ready for me to devour, but I make no move to go to her.

"You may act like an asshole, but you should still celebrate. You're quite charming when you try hard enough." She shrugs as she smiles innocently.

Rising from my seat, I make my way toward her. I've had many women in this room before. So many, in fact, that their faces are merely a blur.

43

None of them return.

Once they walk out the door, they aren't of interest to me anymore. But there's something about the sweet yet fiery girl that makes me want to keep her here, lock her in the bedroom, perhaps even chain her to the bed.

"Don't mistake me for a nice man, Kitten," I tell her. "There's not one nice bone in my body. The moment you deduced I was an asshole, you were correct." We're inches apart, but I make no move to touch her again. If I do, I may not stop.

"Is that why you pay women to come here with you?"

Her curiosity is adorable, and I want more of it. I want to bask in her sweetness. How is a woman who whores herself out so beautiful, so fucking alluring?

"You're a mouthy little thing, aren't you?" I question her. The soft rosy hue on her cheeks turns darker at my question. "Tell me, Kitten." I lean in and allow my lips to whisper over her ear. "Will you lie back on the bed and let me fuck you until you're a boneless mess and when I'm done, leave without questions?"

"Money upfront. You're welcome to throw me out whenever you need to." Her retort is confident, causing me to take one step back, allowing space between us. "And when I leave, I won't be back."

It's what I want. It's the only way I do this… Normally. …But there's nothing ordinary about Katerina. When she first introduced herself as Flame, I knew it was a lie, and I'm shocked she offered up her real name.

"Fine." I pull my cell phone from my pocket before tapping the keys to open the banking app. "Your account number?" Lifting my gaze to meet hers, I raise a brow, waiting for her to give me her details. Once she does, I ensure the payment is made immediately. Her purse vibrates and dings with a notification. I gesture to the bedroom. "Now you can go into the bedroom, take your clothes off, and wait for me. I want you completely naked."

She moves wordlessly, leaving me alone in the living room. Finding Ember's number, I tap out a message, telling him I'll be late. He doesn't respond. He doesn't need to because he knows what I mean.

Stalking into the bedroom, I find the brunette beauty right where I want her. With a smirk, I close the distance between the bed and me. Upon reaching the foot end, my cock throbs as my hungry gaze devours her. She's perfect. Her body is slim, but there's a curve to her hips, and her tiny tits are perky with rosy-colored nipples that are currently hard and peaked.

Her skin is flawless—smooth and creamy—ready

for me to mark with my handprint. When my gaze lands on her pretty pussy, I can't stop the growl that vibrates through my chest. She's almost bare; a dark strip of hair trails from her mound right to her slit, which is currently shimmering with arousal.

"Open your legs."

She spreads her thighs, giving me a delicious view of her perfect little cunt.

"Using your index finger, I want you to stroke yourself."

Slowly, she teases herself with a delicate touch that elicits a whimper from her plump lips, which is pure torture for me because I ache to have my fingers there, inside her, making her moan.

My hand moves to my cock, and I squeeze it while I watch her. I tug my zipper down and free my erection. I match the pace of her hand as it moves over her slick heat. Together, we moan and whimper. Her sounds are the soundtrack to my pleasure, and I could listen to her all day, all night, and never tire of how beautifully melodic she is. If I could record her in the throes of pleasure—like she is now—I'd never need to hear another song again.

Her hips rise up to meet her hand, intensifying the action, and I know it's torture for her just using one finger.

"Dip two fingers into your little cunt," I tell her in a low groan. Her wide eyes meet mine. They're shining with desire so hot, so fucking fierce, I feel it right down to my gut. I haven't touched her, but it's like I can feel her skin beneath my fingertips.

She does as I ask and fucks herself as I jerk my dick. I should do something—touch her, kiss her, or even fuck her, but I can't. She asked me why I pay women to come here, to whore themselves out to me, but she doesn't know how broken I truly am.

She also doesn't know just how special she is to me. I never thought I could do this: be with her in the same room without guilt eating away at me. If she only knew the truth, she'd want to kill me or have me wanting to kill myself, but this right here—having her waiting, ready for me, and not being able to be inside her—it's my own form of torture.

"Come for me," I tell her. "I want to see you find pleasure."

Her body responds. I watch in awe as she fingers herself. Her thighs tremble, her fingers move faster, in and out, and her other hand tweaks her pretty nipples until she's crying out into the large bedroom and I find euphoria in her pleasure.

She didn't call my name.

How I wish she did. There's nothing more I'd like than to hear her screaming as I pinned her to the bed and made her come around my cock. But I didn't, and I can't.

My hand calms its furious stroking, even though I'm still hard. I made a mess on the blanket. I wanted to mark her, to paint her with my seed, but I can't lay claim to her. This is all it is. One night to see her. I did the one thing I promised Ember I wouldn't do.

I almost fucked the girl I'm meant to look out for.

And I know my brother will not be pleased.

KATERINA

WHEN MY EYES FLUTTER OPEN, I FIND THE beautiful man still at the foot of the bed. He's fully dressed, and I wonder if he's even moved since the moment he ordered me to touch myself. I'd gotten so lost in pleasure, I didn't think about anything else.

I trusted that he wouldn't hurt me. Perhaps it's stupid to believe a stranger is truthful, but when I looked into his eyes, I found nothing but honesty. He didn't touch me while I was naked on the bed, not even once. Is there something wrong with me?

Most times, when I've done this, I've never had an inclination to sleep with a client. Of course, they wouldn't refuse, but Ash made me feel at ease while we confessed minor details about ourselves. He could've been forceful and brought me straight to the room, perhaps even pinned me to the bed, but the only contact we had was his fingers teasing me. My gut churns with confusion. However, it steadies when I think about the payment.

The money will certainly pay off the last of the loans, and I'll be able to think about going to college part-time. I'll also be able to pay my rent this week. Shaking my head, I attempt to clear it from the usual worries that replay in my mind. Tonight, here with him, I want to forget all my fears.

He's done something to me, and I can't explain exactly what it is. I wish he wouldn't let me go, but he's made it clear—this is one night only. I know to never get attached to a client. They're traveling businessmen who don't give you forever. There's no diamond ring and house with a white picket fence in my future, and I've come to accept that.

Besides, the pain from the past is ever-present. I can never let it go, and I'm sure no man would want someone who's been damaged to the point of no repair. Love is nothing more than a pretty word they use to advertise a notion of happiness.

The only person I can depend on is me. I know that. I learned it when I was living in a house with a woman who lied about my well-being to keep the social grant flowing into her bank account. And I learned it the day I paid off loans with my college fund.

Ash watches me for a moment. I want him to come to me, hold me, to give me one last bout of affection before I leave. But it's not who he is. I can see it. My chest feels as if pins, and needles are attacking me. My heart, the fucking muscle that's meant to keep me alive, wants to leap into his hands.

Stupidity.

Ash has broken a barrier, one I worked so hard to lock up tight. I let go just this once, and it scares me. He's seen me at my most vulnerable, and I don't know anything about him.

With clients, it's usually mechanical. There is undoubtedly no real passion or desire. It's a job. But with him, there was something else. Something more. Even though I can't describe it, I recognized his affection.

"Get dressed." His gives a low, rumbled order, and my face burns with embarrassment. He turns and leaves me in the bedroom to mull over what just happened. I don't take time to look around. I get dressed without lingering for too long in the room.

When I pass by the bed to exit the space, my gaze lands on the white fluid on the blanket. He did come, which means he was turned on by watching me. I'm not sure why that matters, but for some reason, it puts a smile on my face.

Shaking my head to clear my thoughts, I join him in the living room area where he's perched on the arm of the sofa, staring out toward the city and the dark early morning sky. I'm not sure how long we've been up here, but I'm sure it's nearing sunrise.

"I..." My goodbye tapers off when he turns to regard me. His eyes are dark, conveying heat and longing. He unravels me with a mere glance. This man would break me if I stayed around him for longer than a few hours.

He lifts a tumbler to his lips, swallowing whatever his drink of choice is. I watch as he rises from the sofa, and his steps eat up the distance between us. We're so close, but he doesn't reach for me. I want him to. My body trembles with anticipation, and I long for him to just touch me, even if it's the slightest of caresses, but he remains aloof and detached.

"I'll drive you home," he tells me without so much as an inflection in his voice. No emotion. He's closed off from the man who was in here earlier, questioning me and offering up tidbits about him. Now I'm staring at a stranger.

Nodding, I pick up my purse. "I'm ready." My voice

is small, and the slight tremble in words causes me to chastise myself. I hate sounding weak. It's one of the things I've trained myself not to do. When Isobel first found me, I was nothing more than a meek mouse. But she told me the first thing I needed to learn was not to let shit get to me.

Her motto is *walk in, money up-front, and make them want more.*

And it's worked.

Until now.

Until Ash. If that's actually his real name.

He has no reason to lie to me. I know I'll never see him again, and that's okay with me. As the lie presents itself in my mind, I know I'll want to seek him out.

I should focus on my end goal, not on the man who's made me feel something. I can walk away from someone who could potentially hurt me. He's given me a boost to get out of the pit I'm in. And I'm not sure I'll be able to forget him anytime soon. I know I'll have to.

He guides me to the door and opens it, and we step out into the hallway. Once the click sounds behind me, I don't turn. Instead, I make a beeline for the elevator with Ash hot on my heels. The silence is deafening, but I'm unsure of what to say.

It doesn't take us long to get to the garage where

a slew of expensive cars are parked, waiting for their owners to slip into the driver's seats and take them away. I wish I owned one of those. *One day*, I promise myself. The money Ash gave me will see me through to next week, but after that, I'm back to square one.

Ash pulls open the door to a sleek, onyx-colored Maserati. The windows are blacked out so once I'm in the expensive leather seat, nobody can see me. He joins me a second later, perched behind the steering wheel. Still, he doesn't utter a word.

As we pull out onto the road, he finally asks, "What's your address?"

I recall it in a whisper and watch him press buttons on the screen console. The woman's voice comes through the speakers, informing him to turn right, then drive for a couple of miles before turning left.

I know the city like the back of my hand, and if he took a wrong turn, I'd recognize it immediately. But he doesn't. My prince doesn't steal me away. Instead, he takes me back to the house on the hill which overlooks the lit-up city of Portland. Even though I don't have my own place yet, I'm thankful the view is beautiful from my bedroom window.

"This is me," I tell him, pointing at the exposed-brick

double-story house. The flaking red door beckons me, and before he can say anything, I exit his car, not wanting to linger. The scent of leather sticks to my skin. I don't want to wash it off. Fuck it. I don't want to forget about what just happened. I don't want to forget Ash.

All my clients become faceless strangers, but I know now there's no way I can allow that to happen to him. He's far too beautiful for that. Handsome, yet the keeper holding dark secrets that he hides behind his pretty blue eyes. He didn't say it in so many words, but it's there, concealed beneath his polished exterior.

I don't look back as I make my way to the house. Opening my purse, I close my eyes, willing him to drive away. He doesn't. Instead, I hear the car door slam, and soon his body is behind me, the heat of him cocooning me.

"Tomorrow night. Meet me at the bar at eight," he murmurs so low, I hardly hear him.

Turning to face him, I take him in for a moment before frowning in confusion at his request. "I thought you said—"

"Fuck what I said. Obey me, and I'll pay you another ten grand," he commands in a husky tone. For a young man, he seems far older.

"Okay." I nod.

He doesn't wait for anything more. Turning on his heel, he rushes to his car, and I watch as it peels down the street with a squeal of tires. The engine reminds me of a lion, hungry and ready to feed, and I wonder why he wants to see me again.

He said it was one night. I was certain he was of the mindset he'd made a mistake. And as much as I know I should first check in with Maria, I can't deny how much my heart wants to see Ash again.

That's going to be a problem.

My heart isn't supposed to get involved.

EMBER

STALKING BACK AND FORTH, I CAN'T BRING MYSELF to look at Ashton.

"You've got to be kidding." My voice is tight with anxiety. Of all the things my brother has done, this has got to be the most idiotic of all. He had one job: watch over her. Not take her to his fucking hotel room and make her come.

He doesn't respond, but I know he's not joking. This wasn't the plan, and now I'm having second thoughts. It can only bring pain to all of us. It's a dangerous game, and I know Ash is never going to stop, not until we're all lying in a pile of debris.

I've been in two minds since we set this in motion. But when Ash told me about finding her, I knew there was no way we could walk away. My father always said I was the logical one, the son with his head screwed on right, but now, I feel out of my depth.

I'm still in shock when I meet his gaze. "It took our PI's almost two years to find her. She was lost in the system all this time, and all you do is walk into the damn hotel and—"

"Listen to me." Ash sighs, causing me to halt my pacing and finally meet those familiar eyes. "She's perfect and beautiful, and she's a woman now, but she needs us. Her life has been fucked up for too long, and we can help her." He places the photo on the desk, but I don't look at it. I don't need to see what he did in the hotel room. I don't know if it's anger or jealousy, or perhaps a mixture of both, but my body is vibrating with emotion.

For years, I looked out for Ashton. I kept him safe from pain, from heartache, by not telling him the things our father used to do. When he went out, fucked whores, and came home drunk. He'd fall around the house as if he had lost us all when our mother died. But he had two sons he just didn't want to love.

Yes, on his good days, he was a great father. But it was on those dark days, those nights when he was a broken man that tore our family apart. I see so much of him in Ashton, and it scares me. I want my brother to be happy. To find love. And I wonder if Katerina is the way there.

"Do you think toying with her is going to make our guilt go away?"

Pain flashes in my brother's eyes, and I know I've hit the nail on the head—he's feeling guilty because of what our father did. We need to do this, though. Offer her the assistance she needs to live a normal life. Can any of us ever have that? Perhaps she'll take us up on the agreement that Ash wants to set out for her. She'd be stupid not to accept. But how am I going to tell my brother the one secret I've been hiding for the past year when he's finally happy?

Even though I've dreaded this day for a while, I never could've expected that what happened the night of our birthday would come back to haunt us both. I see the pain in Ash's gaze, and I want to take it away. I want to see his blue eyes glitter with happiness.

The day our lives changed was meant to be a celebration, but our twenty-fourth birthday was a nightmare that still haunts me to this day. Even our father didn't know how to make things right. He tried. He did all he could, but it wasn't enough.

"I think it will ease the hurt that we've all suffered, brother." He spits the words angrily. It's his thing. When he's upset by my prodding his ego, he laces the word with frustration, with rage, and that's typically when I step aside and let him do whatever it is he has planned. But this is far beyond what I ever expected him to want.

My chest aches with guilt, shame, and anger. I don't want her to learn about us. To bring her into our lives and give her the honesty she deserves will break us both. But I can no longer be selfish. If my brother has a chance at some form of forgiveness, I shouldn't deny him that opportunity.

"You really think you can heal a wounded kitten?" My question stills him for a moment, no doubt reminding him of the time when we were just ten years old. Children. Ash and I were playing in the garden. Our mother had been sitting out in the sunshine, watching us run around the grounds when Ash found a cat that had clearly been left to its demise. Wounded and bleeding, he took it in his hands and attempted to comfort it, only for the animal to hiss at him. In his rage, he dropped it on the hard surface of our patio, inadvertently injuring it further and killing it. To this day, we've both never forgotten it.

"I'm not a fucking child anymore, Ember," he bites out. "This was meant to be our project, our game. Once we find her, we give her all she needs, and then we beg for forgiveness." He implores me with wide eyes, waiting for me to refuse him, but I can't. He's my brother—the only family I have left. And I can't see him walk into this alone. No matter how wrong, I think, he is for toying with her. I can't deny I'm intrigued by the girl as well. "Fine."

A smile cracks on his face. It lights his eyes, causing them to shine like jewels. When he's happy, there's a different side to him. But when he's angry, I've seen pure darkness in my brother and at times, it's scared me more than I care to admit.

I wonder if this girl will be the spark that he needs to really change him from the rage-filled person I've lived with all my life into a man who can love.

"I set up a board meeting last night with Fred. He's an asshole, and I want to get rid of him, but for now, I think we'll leave him hanging."

"Was that after you watched her come or before?" I quip, offering Ash a playful smile which he returns. He seems different today, less stressed, which is good. I need to go out later, and I wonder if I should meander by the pretty girl's house. When Ash told me she was living not far outside the main strip, I couldn't help wondering if I should orchestrate bumping into her.

"Smart-ass," he retorts, rolling his eyes. "Before."

The banter between us lightens the mood, and I can't

help but chuckle.

"Anyway, I had to tell you, he's worried we're going to fire him," he informs me. Our father's best friend has been trying to take Addington Corporation away from us since the Will was read.

"If he's not careful, he'll be demoted to a fucking admin clerk," I tell Ash, settling in a chair which overlooks our vast gardens, the same lush green lawn I ran across as a child. When our father died, I wanted to leave, to move out of Addington Hall, but it was Ash who kept me here.

Our mother had passed away years before, leaving us with our father. I miss her every day, but it's my father who taught us how to be the shrewd businessmen we are. Deep down, I yearn for the nurturing love of a woman. I wonder if we would've turned out differently had she lived. Sadness lances my chest, but I push it aside.

I focus on Ashton, who's perched on the edge of the desk on the far side of the room. Our office is a shared space. The large room is decked out with dark mahogany shelving covering one of the walls— books of every kind cover the floor to the ceiling. A window on the adjacent wall overlooks the grounds, and opposite, there's a set of French doors that lead out to a patio and pool area.

The corner of the house is the one area where

we can have our personal space, while also spend time together. With Ashton away most evenings meeting the women he loves to pay, I spend time in here reading and thinking about the uncertain future. Sometimes I wonder if I should just tell my brother the one thing that I've kept from him for too long.

Not yet.

Shaking my head to the dark thought, I try to focus on what I have planned for the day. My love is art. Ash has his music—he's the pianist in the family. Because my father didn't believe there was money to be earned in the arts. Instead, he ensured we each got a business degree.

"I have to get to a meeting. Did you want to tag along?" Ash straightens before stalking toward the window and stopping beside me where I'm perched on the chair.

"No. I need time to think about what I'm going to do the moment I see her, or when I speak to her." My voice cracks and the ache in my chest intensifies. Dizziness hits me suddenly, and I blink a few times before I can look at my brother. Even though I want to go to Katerina and talk to her, fear still niggles in my gut.

"I want to meet with her once more, Ember. Alone. Once I have gauged her reaction to me, we can figure out how to approach her with the offer." My brother is adamant. Perhaps it's for the best that he's doing it on his own because I'm not sure I would be able to walk away.

"Then I want to take her to dinner tomorrow night. You can spend this evening with her, but tomorrow it's my turn," I tell him. "She won't know we're related. I look nothing like you with that mess of hair you call *styled*. I'll call Maria and tell her I'd like company at dinner, and she can set it up." I glance at him, waiting for him to give me an excuse as to why I shouldn't, but he only watches me for a moment, before he smiles.

"Meet her at the hotel, have dinner, delve into the girl's head, and see what she wants. If we're comfortable, we can introduce ourselves on Saturday."

Nodding, I tell him, "Fine. I can do that."

My plan has to work. A date to get her comfortable with me before we finally reveal who we are. If only my brother knew the real reason, I'm doing this. It's for him, it has always been for him.

Ash nods. Buttoning up his jacket, he leaves me in the office to mull over everything I know about the girl. I really should stop calling her that. She's a woman now, but I can't see her as a grown-up yet. It's been two years since I last saw her. I took a step back and left Ash to deal with her, hidden in the shadows until it was my time.

Rising from the chair, I sigh as I make my way through the house. Addington Hall is a monstrosity of eleven bedrooms, a few hectares of lush gardens, and a winding, bricked driveway that takes you off the estate. There's a forest behind the house which leads off to a river. We're nestled on the outskirts of the city, hidden like a jewel in a safe, never to be found.

My mind is a whirl of confusion and anxiety. I want so much to sit Ash down and tell him everything that's bothering me, but I know he's had a lot on his plate since taking over our father's company.

I've always been a loner, and spending my days in the house has become somewhat routine. But there are times I wonder if I should be out there, enjoying my life. It's so fragile; one moment you're living, breathing, and the next, you're no longer here.

I've lost two significant people in my life, and it's pained me in ways I have never confessed to my brother. I wonder how Ash would feel if he lost me. Would he break? I know I'd shatter if he was no longer here.

Love. A precarious emotion that keeps you on the edge, swaying left and right, until one day you fall. Once you do, there's no coming back from it.

I enter my bedroom suite and open the door to my

walk-in closet before stepping inside. The black shelves with mirrored doors offer the space an open feeling. Even though it's not as large as Ashton's wardrobe, there are clothes hung everywhere. Shirts and suits, T-shirts, jeans, shoes, all in black, blue, or gray. I'm not a fan of color. Even my paintings are void of bright shades. There's something beautiful in the darkness. It's a place you can hide. I've suppressed so much already, I don't know how to claw my way out.

My heart hurts. There's a physical pain in my chest, reminding me that I'm going to have to be honest, and that alone will break me.

After pulling out a suit, along with one of the charcoal-colored shirts, I hang them against the door to one of the cabinets. The tie I pick out is silver, which I know will look good against the muted palette.

I have a meeting with two investors this afternoon, and even though it's still early, I like making sure everything is planned, that each suitable item is set out before the time comes. Entering my bedroom once more, I grab my cell phone from the bed and tap in Maria's number. Three rings and I'm greeted by her husky tone.

"Mr. Addington," she says, and I can hear the smile in her voice.

"Maria, I trust you're well?"

"Always. What can I do for you?"

"I'd like a dinner companion tomorrow evening. My brother tells me you have a new girl who's just started?" I enquire, knowing she'll agree. We're some of her best clients—at least, Ashton is.

"Yes. She goes by the moniker Flame."

"Perfect. I'd like to have dinner at the Ivory Hotel at seven tomorrow. She can meet me in the bar area," I inform Maria.

"Of course. I'll schedule her right now."

"Thank you, Maria. Talk soon." I hang up before she can respond.

It's done. I'll meet the precious girl who's got Ash so smitten, and I'll test the waters to see if she would even be willing to accept a proposition from two strangers. I've seen him pursue women before, but it doesn't compare to how happy he looked this morning.

Has she changed? Has she filled out, gotten those womanly curves? Or is she still just a slight waif I could throw onto my bed and have my wicked way with? As much as I think it, I know I won't. Katerina is Ashton's.

Most women think I'm an asshole, and at times I am, but that's until they meet Ashton. I'm the quiet, unassuming brother, who most think of as conceited. Too full of myself. When I step into the room, they fawn over me, giggling and flirting, but that's not what turns me on, so I ignore them until someone catches my eye.

I've never been a fan of going out to have one-night stands with random women. I enjoyed my college years, and I've cared for girls I've been with, but I appreciate a challenge. As time has gone by, my focus has become Ashton's happiness. I've given up on the notion of falling in love, and I'm not concerned about it. I'm content.

It's time for my brother to feel at ease with life, with who he is. It's been years since I've seen him smile, truly grin with happiness. I shove my sweatpants off, then tug my T-shirt up and over my head while I ponder just how I'm going to toy with Ashton to make sure he's as content as I am.

I don't want him to be paying a woman for her company for the rest of his life. And if there's one thing I do know, my brother enjoys when I taunt him. Making it a competition will make him step up his game.

Katerina will be the prize.

I pad into the closet once more in an attempt to get ready for my meeting this afternoon and grab fresh underwear. Back in the bedroom, my mind flits back to

Katerina working as an escort, and try to understand why girls do it, why they sell themselves like that, but I know not everyone is lucky enough to have what we do.

How far down the dark path would I walk if I were forced to? Perhaps not selling my body, but would I be hooked on drugs, stealing? I guess I'll never know. Having a father who provided anything we ever wanted was a privilege, and in all my life, I never took it for granted.

I just wish he was still here to see the men we've become—strong, resilient, and responsible. My eyes burn with emotion threatening to spill, and weariness hits me suddenly, causing me to sit on the bed. I focus on Katerina, on our dinner, on what I know I have to do.

Eighteen. She's still practically a child. And she's had to grow up far too fast.

Sadly, we all did.

I grab my phone and tap out a message to Ash, letting him know I'll be heading into the city to meet with rich assholes who are interested in purchasing stock in the company. I rise on unsteady legs, and head into the bathroom to shower before I start my day.

Once the water is heated, I step under the spray and turn my mind to work.

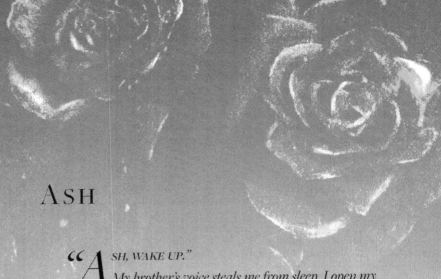

ASH

"*ASH, WAKE UP.*"

My brother's voice steals me from sleep. I open my eyes to find him staring at me as if he's just seen a ghost. Ember has always been a sensitive child, but he seems more stressed out than usual.

"*What's wrong?*"

"*I think Dad is in trouble.*"

That was the moment I knew we were fucked. All the years my father went off the rails, I watched from the sidelines. He wasn't hurting us, and the business was still doing well, but that night changed our lives.

Tonight I'll see her again, and I know at some point, I'm going to have to be honest and tell her who I am, who my father is. But before that, we'll offer her a chance at her dream. Once it's over, I'll have to walk away.

But can I do that?

I should stop Ember from going to meet her. He'll only get attached, and that's not part of the plan. Giving her the opportunity for a new life is what we should be doing; getting involved with her is not.

I shove my office door open and step inside before making my way around the desk. The moment the computer flickers to life, the emails start flowing in. Meeting reminders sound with a ding, but I ignore them all and open the folder on my desktop. Clicking on the image, I open it to full screen and stare at her.

Katerina Nielsen.

Her birthday is coming up soon. She'll be nineteen. Months have passed since I first hired the PI, who finally found her. When he located the pretty girl, I asked him to follow her around. He'd gauged the information I needed. Most importantly he'd hacked into her bank records showing the non-existent balance. And that's when we tracked her down working for Maria.

I know how much she's struggling, and last night when I offered her ten grand, it was nothing. To me, at least. I've been watching her for months. If I had been honest with Ember, I would've told him how much I want her.

I open another folder on my computer, which is

encrypted. Tapping in the password, I click on the police records of the night her family's store went up in flames. No witnesses, no suspects. An accident. I look at them every day as a reminder of how fleeting life is.

"Mr. Addington," Bronwen, my P.A, sticks her head into the office with a bright smile. "Your ten o'clock is here."

"Thank you. I'll be there shortly."

She nods, before shutting the door and leaving me to close both documents and right myself. Time to do some work. As I head out to the boardroom, my head is still filled with how I'm going to pull off all the lies my father left me with.

The day dragged on, and all I wanted to do was finish work early and be at the hotel before Katerina arrives. But it seems I'm the one who's late and she's already here, already nursing a drink. Entering the bar area, I take her in before making my way toward her.

She looks beautiful, and far too innocent sitting waiting for me. I approach her, and settle on a stool, before glancing at her. My hungry gaze takes in the dress that's draped over her slim form. It's black—elegant and classic.

"You look rather lovely," I tell her with a smile, signaling for a whiskey from the barman. A soft blush turns her cheeks darker, and I watch in awe as the pinkish hue travels down her neck.

"Thank you." Her voice is shy. Her gray eyes meet mine, and I'm entranced by her. She's not wearing much makeup, and she doesn't need it. It's the second time I've been in her company, and she's captured my attention more than any woman has before.

"How was your day?" I ask, lifting the newly delivered drink to my lips and taking a sip. The alcohol burns its way down my throat, calming my erratic heartbeat.

"Busy. I had to set up a meeting with the dean in the hope of attending university when the year starts," she says, and I notice the sadness in her tone.

"That's exciting," I offer with a smile. My gaze locks on her trembling fingers as they toy with the glass of wine she's nursing as though it's her last one ever.

"Not sure I'd say exciting," she murmurs, lifting the drink to her lips. She sips the red liquid. "I'm sorry," she says, looking at me. "I didn't mean to sound so morbid about it. I just . . . I'm not sure I'll be able to go to school, at least for another year . . . And I mean . . . Never mind. You don't need to know this."

She stumbles over her words, which makes me grin. There's an underlying pain that I know she hides through the smiles she gifts me with, and I want to wrap her in my arms and tell her it will all be okay. Even though I should offer her solace, I don't. It's not time yet.

"Maybe luck will be on your side," I tell her. "Who knows what life may bring?"

I'm out of my depth. Ember is the one who should be talking about feelings and emotions. I don't deal well with either, and it's clear.

"So, what would you like to do tonight?" she asks, changing the subject.

I can't draw my gaze away from her. Each movement is like a melody, and I fantasize about how I could make music with her body. A gentle caress, a soft kiss, a long, languid lick, and a ferocious nibble. "I'd love to take you somewhere special," I tell her, before swallowing the whiskey and rising from my seat. Offering her my hand, I wait only a moment before she slips her delicate one in mine.

Leading her through the hotel, I find the room which has been set out for me alone. Nobody enters, and none of the guests know it's there. What Katerina doesn't realize is I own this hotel. I own every brick holding this building up. I pull the key from my pocket and slide it into the slot before pushing the door open.

In the center of the room is the most beautiful baby grand piano I've ever laid eyes on. I bought it a year ago, and when I'm here alone, I sit in the room and play to my heart's content. I get lost in the music my fingers make from memory.

The piano I have at home is my salvation, but this? It's my redemption, because it's given me nights of comfort. Each time I thought of Katerina, I promised myself I would bring her here one day. The keys call to me, causing my fingertips to tingle.

"You play?" Kat questions with a smile. Her wide eyes meet mine, and I get lost in them for a moment before nodding.

"I do," I tell her, settling on the stool. Patting the space beside me, I wait for her to sit before asking, "Can I play something for you?"

"Yes, please." Her smile is sweet, her face lit up with excitement.

Turning to the instrument, I linger with my fingers hovering over the keys before I close my eyes and allow them to dance over the ebony and ivories. The melody fills the room, wrapping itself around us, and I let the ballad take hold as the sound resonates against the walls.

Moments pass before I come to the end of the song and open my eyes. When I do, Katerina is watching me with rapt attention. Big gray orbs shimmer with tears, and her plump lips are curled into a grin.

"You're so talented," she murmurs.

"It's not the only thing I'm well-versed in." I chuckle, nudging her shoulder in jest, which lightens the mood in the room after the somber music that filled it only seconds ago.

Her scowl is cute. Her nose wrinkles at me before she responds, "Don't be gross, Ash." Her innocence once again shines through like a beacon on a dark night. The fact that this girl decided that selling herself was a good idea, angers me.

"Just being honest," I tell her with a shrug. "Do you play?" I gesture to the piano.

"A little," she murmurs shyly. I watch her reach for the keys, stroking them reverently as she gazes at them. Then, without warning, she presses down, her fingers lightly dancing along with each key, playing Beethoven's 5th. She doesn't falter. Her body sways as she plays and the curve of her spine along with the column of her slender neck make me lick my lips. She's exquisite.

The song that fills the space is flawless. Watching her get lost in the music turns my body hot with desire. I want to take her, to feel her around me as she plays. Watching her at the piano is like observing a bird take flight, soaring through the sky.

Silence falls the moment she stills. Her body is stationary, and her eyes open. When Kat turns to me, she grins. There's real happiness in her gaze. I want to see that look on her face all the time.

"Someone is hiding secrets from me," I say, tipping my head to the side, allowing my fingertips to trail along her shoulder and reveling in the goosebumps that rise all over her arm.

"I learned to play when I was younger. My mother loved teaching me the melodies. Now that she's gone . . . I mean, I haven't played in such a long time, since she died," she confesses, with a melancholy appearing to replace the now-forgotten contentment. Stormy orbs shimmer with the pain of the past two years.

"I'm sorry. I didn't mean to dredge up painful memories for you," I tell her, placing my finger under her chin to tip her head backward. "I don't like seeing you sad."

"You haven't made me sad." She smiles. "Thinking

of my mother makes me happy. I think what's difficult to come to terms with is knowing I'll never be able to show her how much I've learned."

"I'm certain she's watching over you right now."

She nods. "Probably." Her fingertips linger on the keys, flicking them down in a tune I've never heard before. She continues slowly, playing a wistful song that makes me miss my father.

"That's beautiful."

She shrugs off my compliment as if it's nothing, before telling me, "I've always wanted to study music. I wrote this in my mind a few months ago when I moved in with . . ." Her words taper off, and I realize she doesn't want to give me personal information. Only, I know exactly what she wants to say.

I take this moment to step out of my comfort zone. To see if I can perhaps gauge her reaction to the offer Ember and I have for her. "And if you were awarded a full scholarship tomorrow instead of waiting a year?"

Katerina lifts her hands, causing the song to stop. She doesn't look at me, focusing on the keys instead. Her body is rigid, but then her shoulders sag. She turns her gaze to my curious stare. The corner of her mouth kicks up as she offers me a nod. "I would grab it with both hands."

It's time to talk to Ember. I know what we have to do. After his dinner with her tomorrow night, we'll take her somewhere private and place all our cards on the table. The agreement, the offer, and I hope with all I have that she'll sign.

"Come on. Let's go for a drink and then I'll take you home."

KATERINA

"AND YOU JUST CAME HOME?" ISOBEL QUESTIONS incredulously. Even though we're not very close, she's the only person I have in my corner. The only person I can call a friend.

I'm not sure why I told her about Ash, although I didn't tell her how much he paid me, or the fact that he wants to see me *again* this evening. I gave her just enough to keep her off my back. But she's as excitable as a puppy and hasn't stopped asking questions about him.

Shrugging, I try to act calm like it didn't bother me that he drove me home and asked me to meet him again tonight. I glance at her and respond, "I have a dinner tonight with a client Maria set up for me. I didn't want to be exhausted from staying out late. Also, I was tired."

It's true. This will be my second client date that Maria has booked, and even though I would prefer just being with Ash. My bank balance looks better than it has in a long while, and perhaps soon, I may no longer need to work with Maria.

"Oh, I'm sure you were." Isobel waggles her eyebrows as I lift the mug of coffee to my lips. The strong caffeine is the only thing that's going to get me through today. I'll be able to go into the bank and close the loan account, then I can buy some food to stock up our fridge with the essentials. I'll also need to find a dress for tonight. I'm not sure what the client would like, but knowing I'll see Ash afterward, I want to impress him.

"I'd better head out," I tell Isobel. "I'll see you later?"

She nods. "Yeah, I might be out with a client this evening, but I won't know until he finally messages me. Which will be . . ." She drops her gaze to the cell phone on the kitchen counter. "Well, he should've confirmed already. Maybe his wife is with him, and he can't get away."

"Ha. I'm sure he will be in touch."

A soft blush turns her cheeks pink. "He's sweet, and his wife is a monster." I know she's defending him; it's what she does. This one client has been keeping her busy over the past few months, and I wonder just how much he's paying since she's so smitten with him. One thing she taught me was to never fall for a john, no matter how enticing or how handsome he is. But I have a feeling she's done just that.

"I guess I'll see you tomorrow," I tell her with a shrug. "After the dinner date Maria set up, so I may be home late."

"Are you feeling more confident doing this now?" she asks.

"I think so. As long as the client's payment is large, I'll be closer to my goal." That makes me grin, and she laughs out loud. I recall the name of the client she'd sent through last night. Ember. No last name.

"I'm happy for you, girl," Isobel squeals excitedly. "Perhaps he'll be as hooked on you as Ash is," she winks playfully.

My stomach flip flops at the mention of his name. I shrug it off though because the only thing I have to focus on is enrolling in school, even if it's part-time. When Ash asked me last night if I'd ever take someone up on their offer, I knew I would. Stupidly, I was hoping he was about to say he'd help me. I'm not sure why I've allowed my emotions to get involved where he's concerned, but I have.

"If they're paying, I'm dating. Anything else can take a back seat." Even as I tell her this, the thought of Ash having feelings for me lingers in my mind.

"You're learning. Just don't ever fall in love," Isobel

warns me once more.

That thought settles like a lead weight in my stomach when a brief flash of Ash's face invades my mind. It reminds me of how my chest ached when he dropped me off at home in the early hours of this morning. I'd wanted to spend more time with him, even though I knew it would be a mistake.

"I know, girl, I know," I tell her. "I have to go." Going on the date tonight might allow me to put Ash out of my mind for a little while.

"See you later, babe." She smiles, offering me one of her sly winks, which I know means she thinks there's more to my story than I'm letting on. And to be fair, she's not wrong.

I've sold my soul, and there's no going back. The handsome devil who paid for my time is a danger to my emotional state. Nobody has ever been genuinely kind to me, and as wary as I am around him, I can't stop my heart from beating wildly when he's near.

My parents always taught me to be careful of strangers. To be independent, and to never take anything at face value. And I need to heed their advice now more than ever. It's easy to get swept up in the excitement of having wads of cash coming in.

It's almost been a year since I graduated high school, and college is finally looking like a prospect. But nothing in life comes for free, and I need to keep my wits about me.

Everything and everyone has a price. I need to make sure mine is high. I'm worthy of happiness, of a normal life, and I shouldn't settle for what I have now.

But as much as I keep reminding myself of that fact, there's nothing to stop me from smiling when I step into the building to pay my rent for the next two months.

Ash's money has been the most a client has ever given me. Over the first couple of *dates*, I've only ever been offered a grand—one thousand for an evening at an event—and I've accepted because it's the quickest way to get out of the rut.

The moment I meet with the dean and can pay for my tuition will be the day I finally feel proud of who I am.

Right now, I'm riddled with guilt at what I have to do to get there. The anxiety that claws at me each time I have a client has me worried that one day, something will happen to me.

When I lost my parents, then my home, I didn't think I'd make it to eighteen, let alone to the position I'm in now. The lawyer who tried to fight for me to live in my parents' home with a guardian present lost the case. He tried every loophole he could find, short of offering to adopt me himself, he gave me hope for a while.

I'm not sure what happened to him. When I was thrown into the system, I didn't see him again. It's odd how a stranger can change your life without even knowing it. The reason I'm not dead in a ditch somewhere is that he told me to never give up.

With every ruling, he would pat me on the shoulder and tell me things would work out. He was so sure of his words that he instilled confidence in me that I never let go of. And even when I was in the foster home, I kept replaying his advice in my mind. A surrogate father of sorts, he gave me something I needed at the time—surety.

When I told Ash this life was temporary, I meant it. And when I told him I'd gladly grab any opportunity to study, it was the most honest I'd been in a long time. I gave myself a year to save up, a year of doing this bullshit, and as my time ticks on, I wonder if twelve months will be enough. Hopefully, if I can see Ash a few more times, he'll be able to help me.

My plan is simple.

The state took my family home, and I know it's been empty for years. I intend to study, work my ass off, and one day, I want to buy that house back, maybe even raise a family in the place I grew up in. There's something special about it. Smiling, I shove my hand in my purse and feel the envelope I've been hiding for months—the letter burning a hole in there reminds me I need to respond, but I can't. Not yet. Even though they're offering me a half-scholarship, I need time to make up the rest of the tuition. For now, I ignore the burn and grin at the bank clerk as I approach the desk.

This is it.

One step forward.

I pray there won't be two steps back.

KATERINA

THE RESTAURANT AREA I'VE BEEN ESCORTED TO IS exquisite. They've seated me close to the back of the space, so when I look up, I can see every corner of the room. The hostess let me know my date requested for me to be at this particular table. I'm nervous. It's like what I imagine being on a blind date is like.

Even though this is purely professional, I still feel anxious. What if we don't connect? What if I bore him and he complains to Maria? Or would we enjoy each other's company over dinner? My stomach is fluttering with nerves. I attempt to calm myself with deep breaths, but it doesn't work.

I take in the various tables dotted around the large room. It's not busy yet, and I can't help noticing the people already seated—men and women whose appearances scream *money*. Their drinks are served in sparkling crystal, and the place settings are exquisite with shiny silver cutlery. Candleholders which reflect the light from the chandeliers above sit in the center of the tables.

I feel out of place. Up until my parents died, I had been comfortable. But the clientele here are all upper class. From their jewelry to their expensive clothes, I can almost smell the wealth in the air.

I can certainly act the part, but deep down, I know the dress I'm wearing is from two or three seasons ago. My shoes aren't brand new and shiny. My jewelry is merely costume gems I found at a thrift store, and I haven't been to a hair salon in years.

I focus on the glass of water in front of me, wondering what my parents would think of me if they were here right now. I've only ever wanted to make them proud. My eyes prick with tears when I think about my mother's advice: *never let anyone tell you that you can't do something*. It was a mantra she drummed into my head since I gave up on ballet classes.

I'd wanted to learn to dance the longest time, but I just wasn't good. My real love was for music, art, and when I found that out, Mom supported me. The nights she sat with me, teaching me to play the piano, the Sunday mornings she would take me into the garden when we'd paint flowers. All those are merely memories now, and each day, I'm afraid they'll just disappear into a pile of ash.

I shake my head, taking a sip of the cold liquid from my glass. I sweep my gaze toward the doorway only to have my focus fall on the man at the entrance. He enters the room, and all eyes turn toward him. Mine eat him up in a quick gobble, noting his dark suit and silver tie. His shirt is a crisp black material. He nears me, and I rise to greet him with a smile.

"You're looking lovely, Flame. I'm Ember," he tells me before placing a kiss on both my cheeks. His hand holds onto my arm, causing my stomach to flip-flop and nervous energy to course through me.

"Thank you. It's lovely to meet you, Ember." My voice is raspy when I respond, and I realize the anxiousness is getting to me. I attempt to swallow it down, hoping I can calm my erratic heartbeat.

Ember gestures to the chair, holding onto the back of it as he waits for me to settle in. With his green eyes pinned on me, watching me, I offer him a smile, just like I did when Ash looked at me in the same way. "I wasn't sure what you wanted me to wear, so . . ."

"You're perfect," he tells me before seating himself opposite me. "I don't do this often, but when I saw you on the website, I called Maria and booked dinner. I'd hoped this would offer us an opportunity to get to know each other."

"I'm . . . I must say this is still very new to me. I mean—"

The waitress appears at that moment, interrupting my response to take our orders. I allow Ember to choose for me since he seems so confident naming a specific bottle of wine I'd never heard of. With a nod of agreement from my side, he selects the food as well.

Once we're alone, he glances at me. "I hope you don't mind me taking the liberty, Flame." His smile lights up his face as he watches me intently.

"I don't mind. Thank you," I tell him. "I'm not familiar with the wines here." Hoping he doesn't notice my little white lie as I try to appear more worldly than I really am. His smile doesn't give him away, so I lift the water and take a sip, praying it will calm my nerves.

I didn't think being here with a stranger like this would be too difficult, but then again, I wasn't expecting him to be so handsome. So young. He looks to be about Ash's age, and I wonder for a moment why men like him need to pay women to date them.

The waitress brings our drinks and the starter, which

looks incredibly delicious. Ember takes the bottle from the pretty girl and gestures for her to leave before he pours wine into both our glasses. He seems so confident, and for a beat, I'm jealous of the ease with which he moves. If I could just have an ounce of that grace and elegance, I would be much more comfortable. But then, perhaps men like innocent, nervous, fluttery girls.

Ember lifts his glass to make a toast. "To making new friends," he says, his mouth curling into a wolfish smile. There's something familiar about him, but I can't quite put my finger on it. I shake it off and try to focus on the *here and now.*

After clinking my glass with Ember's, I take a sip of the smoky, spicy liquid before I look into his eyes. "Will you tell me why a guy like you would need to pay a girl to have dinner with him?" I question. It's the same one I asked Ash, and I wonder just what it is about these men that makes them want to close themselves off to something real.

"My life hasn't afforded me a chance to venture into a relationship. Not right now anyway," Ember tells me with a melancholy tone in his voice. There's a faraway look in his gaze which makes me curious when he continues, "People are flippant about emotions, about connections.

This way, I don't need to promise something I can never give."

"It sounds like you're already set on walking away from someone before you've given them a chance," I counter, watching him while I sip my drink. The nerves that had attacked me earlier seemed to have settled, and for the first time tonight, I don't feel like a paid escort, but rather, a girl on a date with a man.

He shrugs, but appears to ponders my words because he doesn't respond immediately. There's something almost regal about how he holds himself which further intrigues me.

"Perhaps I have." He smiles. "I've just learned that over time, everyone leaves, so you can't get attached." Ember picks up an olive from the bowl, sucking it into his mouth. I can't help licking my lips at the sight of his tempting mouth wet with the sauce.

"Sometimes people can surprise you," I tell him, picking up a small green fruit the same color as his eyes. His gaze falls to my mouth, observing me as I enjoy the bitter flavor of the sauce.

There's a heavy silence in the air before he responds, "They can. As did you, Flame. I'm rather intrigued by you." He sips his wine. "Tell me what your hobbies are? What are you passionate about?" he questions, arching a chestnut eyebrow. Ember sits back and watches me intently. He's waiting for an answer, and I want to give it to him.

"I didn't think you'd want to learn too much about me since I'm only here for the night," I challenge, causing his eyes to shimmer with mischief.

"Call me curious," he smirks. The corner of his mouth quirking as he regards me.

"My passion is music. I learned to play the piano at an early age."

He tips his head to the side, his gaze locked on mine. "Lovely. And do you still play?"

"I haven't for a long while. I don't have one at home to practice on. Although I did get a chance to play last night."

"Oh?" This seems to interest him, and he leans forward placing his forearms on the table, and his fingers tangle together. "Did you enjoy it?"

"I always enjoy creating music." I smile, lowering my gaze to the table for a moment before meeting his heated stare. "What about you?"

His gaze flickers with something—but it's gone before I pinpoint it—as he responds, "I paint. More than I should, less than I'd like."

"I'm a fan of art as well. There's always a complex

emotion an artist portrays in the use of color, brush strokes, and canvas." Our conversation makes me smile.

"Ah, now you've got me thinking of getting you to come and paint with me one day, Flame," he chuckles, twirling his glass on the table, causing the wine to splash against the edges.

"Katerina," I offer. "My name is Katerina." I may never see him again, so I give him my real name because as much as I want to hide behind my moniker, it doesn't feel natural. Honesty—it's the one thing I've always promised myself I'd give where and when I can. I can't explain my need to tell him the truth, but it's there.

He smiles and once more, I'm hit with the feeling that he's somehow familiar. But I can't cement the notion as to why or how.

"Katerina, do me the honor of spending a day with me in my studio?" He tips his glass, clinking it on mine before finishing the last swill of red liquid, swallowing it down, and I'm entranced by the bopping of his Adam's apple. "Say yes," he implores with a cocky grin that makes my cheeks heat.

EMBER

SHE'S UTTERLY BREATHTAKING. MY EYES DON'T leave her, not for one minute.

"Just one day, Katerina," I utter, caressing her name like it is the most beautiful thing I've ever heard. It fits her perfectly. Her eyes shimmer as she regards me critically. She shouldn't trust easily, but I don't look away because I want her to see the honesty in my eyes.

A small smile dances on her lips before she responds, "I'll think about it." Her words are raspy. "I guess it could be part of the job."

"It is. Trust me, I'm only offering an invite."

"I learned never to trust people, but . . ."

"But you feel you could trust me?"

She nods.

"And why is that?" I sip my wine, watching her. She's an enigma. So strong, so beautiful and resilient.

"I don't know, to be honest." She lifts her gaze from the glass to meet mine. "I guess I'm trying to see the best in people and hoping that they don't hurt me." She shrugs as the waitress sets our mains on the table.

The steaming plates of cheesy risotto smell delicious, but my appetite is not for the food, but rather for more information about the woman sitting across from me. "You've got an interesting outlook on people, Katerina. Not everyone is worthy of trust." I voice my observation. "You seem far too grown-up for those youthful features."

She blushes. The pink darkening her alabaster skin makes her face glow. A shy smile plays on her lips, and I can see why my brother is so enamored with her. "I had to grow up fast."

Pain laces her words. They grip my heart, and I have to swallow my wine to keep from telling her I know. Secrets kept are lies not voiced.

"Anyway, tell me about you. If you'd like," she suggests, gesturing toward me.

"Mm, where to start . . . I'm one of two boys in our family," I confess. "My brother is the eldest by about . . . two minutes."

Her eyes widen at my words.

"And he tends to act like an asshole most times, but

I put up with it because I love him. However, it's a secret because I like to keep him on his toes." I wink at her conspiratorially, causing her to blush again. The hue of pink darkening to a soft red looks stunning on her cheeks.

"Your secret is safe with me." She smiles. "That is, if I ever meet him." She sounds intrigued by my snippet of information, which makes me curious to see her reaction when Ash and I confess.

"What are your future plans?" I question, knowing Ash threw something similar to her last night.

Her sigh is a soft sound which captures my attention. "I'd love to go to school, but I need to do a bit of saving before that happens. I've given myself a year to ensure I can cover the tuition."

"You have no one to help you?" I don't know why I ask when I know the answer. But perhaps I just want to hear it in her words. She has nobody in this world but Ash and me, and I intend on making sure she sees her dreams come true. Even if I can't be around to witness them. My food is forgotten, my focus on the girl who's had to become an adult far too soon.

"No," she tells me sadly before she forks some risotto into her mouth. Kat chews slowly, and a soft moan rumbles in her throat. The sound acts like an aphrodisiac—sensual and erotic.

Her movements are like art—gentle, like a sweeping brushstroke, but alluring like bright color screaming at me from a canvas.

Once she swallows her mouthful, she smiles. Squaring her shoulders confidently, Katerina continues, "But I've learned to be independent, and I think my parents would be proud of the person I've become. Not for the work, I've taken on, but by being responsible. And that I'm alive and healthy."

Nodding, I wonder what my father would say about Ash and me. Would we please him with how we've turned out? Ash running the company, while I'm working at the university tutoring students.

She looks at me, then asks, "Are your parents—"

"They're both dead," I interrupt, not wanting to talk about my father, and also not wanting to remember my mother. Missing her has been a pain I have carried for a long time. And whenever I think about her, it's as if I'm still there, watching her take her last breath

Losing a parent isn't easy. You think they'll be there to see you grow up, to watch you turn from child to adult and offer you the love and nurturing you need. Without them, I've become accustomed to offering my love to my brother. It's been enough. And now it seems I want Kat to experience that love as well.

I know Katerina understands. More so than anyone can. She's not had a family for two long years, and I wish I could give her one. Even just being her friend would offer her some form of comfort.

"I'm sorry, I didn't mean to—"

"It's okay," I tell her, gulping down the Merlot before pouring another generous glassful for us both. "It's been a long time since I've spoken to anyone about them, either of them. I just prefer not to."

"I get it." She nods.

We eat in silence, but I can't stop glancing her way every few seconds. She's holding all the power in our exchange because I'm intrigued. The innocence she still holds, even though she's been through so much in her short life, is incredible. I want to tell her about my pain, to admit who I am.

She deserves happiness. And I'm going to make sure she gets it.

I sit back, pushing my plate away, ready to learn more about Katerina. She finishes her dinner and looks at me, offering a sweet smile. Tentatively, she picks up her glass and tips it my way. "Thank you for dinner; it was delicious.

To putting the past behind us and moving forward, wherever that may lead."

"I can agree with that." I clink my glass against hers. The soft lyrical sound is the only thing I hear because, for a moment, I want a future. But most of all, I hope this beauty gives my brother a fighting chance. Each time I look at her, I pray that she'll be his beacon within the darkness I know is about to take over his life.

"So, Katerina. I hope you don't mind me calling you that?"

She shakes her head. "Not at all."

"Tell me more about your love of art and music?" I ask.

"I learned piano when I was much younger. My mother taught me to play." She regards me. "Painting was always something I could get lost in at night when I wasn't allowed at the instrument. My parents would be in bed by nine, and I would spend another hour creating colorful canvasses."

Even though I knew what she'd say, I savor having something in common with her. "I'd like to see your work sometime?"

"Perhaps."

I turn the conversation toward her favorite artists

and revel in the ease with which we spend the evening in each other's company. The night turns late, and when I glance at the time, I notice it's almost eleven. "I'd better drive you home." I rise from my seat after making sure the bill is paid, and the waitress has been tipped.

"Oh, you don't have to."

Shaking my head, I insist, "I want to."

I've already made up my mind about her, about offering her the agreement. The moment we step foot outside the restaurant, I know I'm going to head home and tell Ashton we need to tell her, help her. Anything to make her life better than the shit show it is now. And I have a feeling he'll agree.

When the car pulls up to the sidewalk outside her house, she turns to look over at me. "Thank you, this was . . . It was a lovely evening."

"I should be thanking you for keeping me company," I respond easily because it's true. I usually only spend time with my brother over dinner. Katerina has been a breath of fresh air and how much I enjoyed tonight was rather unexpected. "Perhaps we'll see each other soon."

"I hope so."

I want so badly to offer her a fairy-tale kiss goodnight, but I don't. I'm not here for that. I'm here to ensure that she'll fit with Ashton. I'm not the one who needs her most; my brother is. And as much as I think she's stunning, beautiful, I know I can't do anything about it.

"Sweet dreams, princess," I utter as I watch her enter the house. I turn to my driver. "Take me home."

And in silence, we head back to the Addington mansion which has become a semblance of salvation for me.

For months I've been wondering how to confess to Ash about what's troubling me, but I know with Katerina by his side, it will ease the blow of the decision I've made. He might hate me for a time, but he'll realize it was for his own good.

I've only ever wanted the best for him, and this is going to be my ultimate gift.

ASH

"And this is why you're not running the company, and I am," I tell the old man. My anxiety has skyrocketed today, and this board meeting has been the cause of it. Ember sits at the opposite end of the table, watching me silently. My brother has always been the quiet one, whereas, as a child, I would be running around the house, screaming bloody murder.

"Mr. Addington," Frederik Larson says in an icy tone as he pins me with a heated glare. "With all due respect—"

"Yes, respect," I interrupt him. "That's something I'd be grateful for in this meeting. My decision is final. We'll refuse the expansion of this hotel chain into Miami for now. We don't need to be worried about that when the L.A. and Chicago sites are teetering on edge. My father wanted the business to profit, and I'm not putting the Addington name on the line if shit goes south."

Dad bought the chain with his brother over ten years ago, before they had a falling out and my uncle decided he didn't need family. They turned the broken-down shitholes that were about to shut their doors and turned them into four-star hotels that were doing well until my father listened to Larson five years ago. Since my father's death, this asshole has been trying to drive the business into the ground.

Not on my watch.

"Our investment in the chain will remain as is. Shut down Miami, put our focus into the hotels we have now, and when we have them turning a profit, we'll talk about expansion. Am I understood?"

There's a murmur along the table. On each side sit five men old enough to be mine and Ember's fathers. But none of them would ever fill his shoes. At times, I doubt I can.

"Mr. Addington," Frederik utters, "I'm sorry if I overstepped," he says, offering a solemn nod. "We'll make sure to focus on the L.A. and Chicago sites. I'll fly out in the morning, and when I return, I'll give you a report."

"Perfect. Is there anything else I need to look at?"

"Will you be meeting with the Dean this afternoon?" Heinrich Lincoln, the Chief Operations Officer, questions.

"Yes," I tell him. "Ember and I will be working with Dean Reginald to set up the interviews for our scholarship applicants for the upcoming year."

Each year, my father gifted two scholarships to promising students. He'd meet with them, interview them to find out their goals and dreams, and he'd decide if he was willing to back them. Once they completed their studies, they were free to work for us, or they would be sent to work at my uncle's law firm. Even though the brothers hardly spoke, they ensured the staff, students, and business associates weren't left out in the cold.

This year, I'll be meeting with the prospective candidates, and I look forward to it. Taking over from my father wasn't easy. Even though Ember is here to assist me, I'm the one who was named CEO, with my brother as my partner. But I know deep down this isn't what he loves. He prefers tutoring at the university.

"Is there anything else?" I ask again, glancing around the room at the men I now lead.

A murmur of "no" rounds the room, and I dismiss the board. Once Ember and I are alone, I settle in my chair at the head of the table and watch him. We've been close all our lives. We don't bicker like other siblings do instead gravitate around each other. We offer advice when needed and solace when there was none after losing our parents.

My brother's an empath. But I'm a coldhearted bastard. We couldn't be more different if we tried. The problem about my brother's affliction is that whether he's around me or not, he knows how I feel; the agony in my chest is his. That's why I go out and fuck random women. I take whores to a hotel room and get lost in their bodies because it's the only way I can deal with my pain.

My brother is good. He's beautiful and pure down to his core, and sometimes I wonder if I weren't around if he'd be different. Perhaps my iciness makes him warm. At least, that's what I'd like to believe. Who knows?

"You handled it well." He smiles, causing his dimples to peek through.

Shrugging, I close the folder on the table before me. "It's what Dad would've wanted. He was the only one I could trust to know what to do, but now—"

"You have to trust yourself, Ash." Ember always finishes my sentences, my thoughts. He's a part of me; my other half. He's in my soul.

"Why are you so down? I can feel you're—"

"I want her, Ember."

He's as surprised by my confession as I am. When I meet his gaze, I see it—the confusion swirling around in those green depths.

"You may want her, but she might not want you," he warns me. "Father would roll over in his grave." His words are gritted out, and it's the first time in a long time that I've seen the rage inside him. Under the calm exterior, I know my brother has darkness. It runs in our family. We have more money than God and more power than Satan himself. And we've always used it to our advantage, but when my father bought the hotel chain and built Addington & Associates, he gave back. Like the scholarships. It was his way of thanking the universe for what we have.

I think over time, when my father realized how fucked up our family truly was, he renounced the rules my grandfather laid down and created his own life. And I respect that, but I know there's simmering violence that still trickles through my veins. I'm an Addington, and I always will be.

"I want her, and there's nothing you can do to stop me," I tell Ember, rising from the chair. I pin him with a glare. He knows if I want to do something, I'll do it. I'm stubborn, and my brother has had to put up with it all my life.

"I'm not going to stop you, Ash," he tells me easily. "But I want to be there tonight when you show her the offer. I want to see her agree to this because forgive me, brother, I care for her as much as you do."

"Are you sure?" I question Ember, shocked at his revelation. Unease settles in my gut, but my need for the girl is far too fierce. "This girl is our salvation. This is what we need to do to make sure the past is finally laid bare, and then we can hopefully get some form of forgiveness for not being there for her sooner. Our game is over once she signs the agreement. We'll have to find a way to tell her the truth."

Ember shakes his head before responding, "Not yet. We can't risk her telling us to go to hell. If she knows the secret we hold, she might run."

He's right. Katerina can't know until she's in too deep.

"She'll enjoy the perks but walk away unscathed from the blaze. We can offer her a place to stay, get her studies underway, and allow her to see what she could have."

My brother's mind is obviously calculating all the ways this could and couldn't work. I observe him as his expression morphs from that of the serene and calm brother, I know to a tense and nervous man out of his element.

"Ember, I think I should—"

"Ashton, offer her something she can't refuse, but be

careful of emotions getting in the way. She needs to focus on her career, her future."

"What if I can be her future?" I counter.

"Maybe you can." His olive-green eyes meet mine with confidence shining in them. "I believe you could make her happy, but she needs to decide."

As much as I want to deny him, my brother is right. I can do this. If the pretty little kitten wants to play, we can offer her all the dreams she currently sees as out of reach. And if I can find it inside myself to let Katerina in, maybe I can offer her something more.

KATERINA

I STARE AT THE PHONE SCREEN IN SHOCK. The fluttering in my stomach awakens with a vengeance, and I realize I'm smiling like a fool at the words I read and re-read.

"Tonight. Ivory Hotel at eight. I look forward to seeing you, Kitten."

My response is tapped out quickly. *"And where pray tell did you get my number from?"*

"Your boss likes money. Let's just say I persuaded her."

I need to talk to Maria. Even though I don't mind Ash having my details, she shouldn't be giving them out. Although my frustration at her burns hot, I'm excited at the prospect of seeing him again. The words he sent are ingrained in my mind. And soon, nothing else I try to read even registers. Forcing my mind back to the website in front of me, I read through the minimum requirements for entry to Silverwood University with a half-paid scholarship.

Once I've gotten all the information I need scrawled in my notebook, I log off the computer and wave at the lady behind the counter. I could use my phone, but I like being out amongst people. This morning, I woke up and decided on a latte and an hour doing research.

I'm hoping I'll be able to buy a laptop soon. As I walk down the main road toward home and also the hotel, I think about last night's date. I enjoyed my short time with Ember. He's handsome, charismatic, and I wonder if he'll ask to see me again.

He doesn't make me feel the way Ash does, but the way Ember listened, acted as if he were genuinely interested in what I had to say, was refreshing.

I've never had a boyfriend, and in the past week, I've met two men who've captured my attention. I know I shouldn't grow attached because people always leave. And they're clients paying for my time. I need to remember with Ember it's not real friendship, and it's certainly not a real relationship.

I think my excitement stems from just having someone to talk to. Someone who has similar interests to Ember and me seems like the type of person I could perhaps learn from. He mentioned he teaches art; maybe he'll be able to help me once I've gotten back on my feet.

When I reach the house, I head up to my bedroom and turn on the stereo. Music filters through the speakers, and I open my closet. I'm not sure what to wear. The hotel is fancy, and my heart sinks when I look at the old clothes that hang before me.

Ash has seen me in black and the orange one. The charcoal colored dress is perfect for this evening, so I pull it out and drape it over the mattress. I have a pair of silver sandals which I can wear, and perhaps some dangly earrings I got from Isobel.

A dark gray and silver ensemble will look classy, yet the styling of the garment is sexy, and that's the way I'd like Ash to see me. Glancing at the time, I note that I still have an hour before I have to shower and get ready, so I settle on the mattress and pull out the small box of photos from under my bed.

After unlatching the lock, I open the lid and lift the pictures from inside. The first one is of my parents sitting at a table on their wedding day. Another is of Mom and me at the piano. Dad was the photographer, watching us play.

My eyes burn with tears when I think about not having them here to give me advice. To listen to me talk about a boy I like, about a class I hate or love, or even just to hold me when I'm feeling alone.

Because right now, in this small single room, I feel so alone. I blink, and salty emotion trickles down my cheek. I go through all the photos, each picture reminds me of where I've come from, what I've been through, and what I've lost.

I shouldn't have opened the box now, but I needed to remember why I'm doing this. The reason I'm going to meet a man who's going to pay me for the evening—to ensure my future isn't as bleak as my past.

The smiling faces who look back at me are strangers now. I can no longer hear my mother's voice. It's faded from my mind, and I can't recall my father's laugh. Slowly, they're slipping away, and the more time that passes, the sooner they'll be gone, and I won't have anything to remember them by but my photos.

"I'll make you proud, Mama," I murmur to the photo. My gaze lands on the man in the background, the father I didn't really know because he never told me the truth. "I wish you had been honest with us, Papa, and told us you were struggling."

Perhaps my father was trying to be strong for my mother and me. He was always a hero in my eyes, and I suppose I'd put him on a pedestal he couldn't topple from.

"I love you both," I tell them. "I'll be out of here soon, sooner than I expected, and I won't be stuck doing this forever. I have a life ahead of me, and I promise you I'll make it."

With conviction, I rise from my bed before packing away the photos and heading to the bathroom to get ready for this evening.

The hotel is within view, and I smooth my hands down my thighs as I make my way toward it. The large glass doors slide open, and I walk inside the entrance foyer. Glancing to the left, I take note of myself in the mirror which is set behind enormous plant pots. Smiling at my reflection, I turn and stroll forward. I feel comfortable for the first time in my life. My choice of dress this evening gives me the confidence I lacked before. It may be *last season*, but I feel like a million dollars.

The scooped material falls to the base of my spine, and the neckline is high, offering no glimpse at my meager cleavage. Thin straps slink down my back, and the hemline swooshes along my ankles. The shoes I'm wearing are silver, matching the edging of the dress.

I decided to leave my curly hair hanging loose, framing my face. I've applied a light dusting of blush, along with a dark catlike flick of eyeliner.

As soon as I enter the lounge area, my stomach somersaults and my eyes track each person, looking for the handsome young man with the bluest eyes I've ever seen. His unruly golden hair was so tempting, I wanted to tangle my fingers through the locks, but I held back.

Settling myself at the bar, I choose my favorite chair in the corner, so I can see everyone who enters and leaves. I'm not sure why I'm so nervous, but I am. Stupidly, I feel as if I'm on another date, which I know should not be something I even think about.

He didn't explain what he had in mind for this evening. Perhaps tonight he will want to do more than just watch me writhe on his bed. If he does, he may be sorely disappointed. My lack of experience won't earn me another ten thousand.

Ash is paying for my time, perhaps even my body, and I know the excitement I'm feeling should be tamped down. But just for a moment, I want to feel like a normal girl. Not someone who sells their time and company to pay their rent.

"Can I get you something?" The barman glances at me, and the moment I meet his gaze, he smiles. "Oh, Ash said to get you anything you'd like."

My mouth falls open, before I question, "Really?"

"Yes, he called ahead. He'll be here soon. What would you like to drink?"

Smiling at the thoughtfulness of the man who's messing with my rules, I place my order. "I'll have a club soda please?"

"Sure." He turns and leaves me, and I watch him open the fridge, and fill a glass. I would prefer a glass of wine, but I'm nervous about ordering it since I don't have my identification tonight. When the barman sets the glass of red wine down alongside the one that I ordered, he offers a nod, "orders from the boss."

Boss? I want to ask, but he's gone before I have a moment.

I lift the glass and take a long sip of the bubbly liquid, wondering if I should just drink the red alcohol Ash ordered for me. My father used to allow me a sip of his wine with dinner. He would always have a glass of red. I smile as I think about the times, he'd explain the notes he detected—some were fruity, others smoky, or even spicy.

My chest aches as I blink back the tears again. I

wonder if the pain from missing them will ever abate. Dabbing at my eyes, I glance at the room again before sighing.

Tipping the glass against my lips, I take a sip, reveling in the delicious flavors assaulting my taste buds. The fruity, yet wooded hints are amazing, and I can't help a soft moan of pleasure tumbling from my lips.

"If you make those sounds over a glass of wine, what might you do once I fuck you?" The soft, yet sensual whisper comes from behind me, causing me to whip my head toward the voice. Ash is standing there, looking sure of himself as he offers me a wolfish, playful smirk.

Dressed in a white button-up shirt, with a black suit jacket, and a red tie, he settles beside me. His hair is messy, and I wonder if he ever brushes it. I note how the colors differ, the dark hue lightening as it gets to the tips. A golden halo. That's what it looks like.

"You're welcome to find out if you'd like," I flirt with him, offering a seductive smile. I want to play this game to give him a bit of what he provides in spades.

"I will find out soon enough, Flame," he says, using the name I gave him on our first night. I'm thankful he doesn't utter my real name, which I stupidly confessed to him. I'd never told anyone who I was before that, but I had a feeling he needed to trust me, and that was the only reason I told him. At least, that's what I convince myself.

"Did you have a good day?" I ask, turning to face him as I sip my wine.

"It's been rather tedious, to be honest," he sighs, before signaling the barman, and I notice he doesn't voice his order. The man serving knows what he likes.

"Do you come here often?"

He darts his deep blue eyes to mine, and something flickers in them. As if I've asked a question, he's not comfortable answering. Just like I did when I asked about his birthday.

"Occasionally my clients want to have business meetings here, so I've been here a few times," he offers. Picking up the tumbler the bartender left on the counter, he sips the amber liquid, not meeting my gaze again. Instead, he fiddles with the coaster, turning it in circles while I ponder his response.

"I see." I drink my wine, unsure of why our conversations start off well and then turn sad, or uncomfortable.

"Finish your drink. We're going up to the room," he tells me but doesn't look my way. His abruptness causes me to pause for a moment before I down the last mouthful of flavorsome liquid. Rising from the chair, I wait for him to gulp down his whiskey, then he guides me to the elevator with a tender touch to my lower back.

We walk in silence. There's nothing to say because it's clear why we're both here. To get lost in the fantasy. As if I were Cinderella and the prince was taking me to his castle. I can't help smiling at the silly thought, and I catch Ash's gaze when we reach the mirrored elevator.

"Something funny?" he asks while pushing the button to call the car. As soon as the *ding* sounds, the doors slide open, and we step into the small space.

"Just thinking," I tell him, not bothering to turn his way. Whenever I look into the depths of his eyes, I get lost, and it's dangerous to allow myself to fall into the promises he holds there.

"A penny for your thoughts," he says.

We're inches apart. I can feel the warmth of him prickling along my skin, and I want to reach out and touch him, or perhaps, I want him to touch me. To acknowledge the fire burning between us.

"Nothing that you need to worry about," I tell him softly.

It's strange; this is our third meeting, and each time we're together is more intoxicating than the last. At eighteen, almost nineteen, I haven't spent so much time around one man. Especially, someone, I would consider a relationship with, but this feels close to what I would've thought it would feel like.

Only if we were dating, he wouldn't be paying me large sums of money. *Mom, I wish you were here to offer me comfort in my confusion.* I blink back the emotion that fills my eyes and swallow the lump in my throat.

I'm more nervous now than I was the first night I came upstairs with Ash.

When we finally step out into the hallway, I follow him toward the familiar door. The *click* of the keycard sounds louder than it should; it booms in my ears. He ushers me inside and there I find a man sitting on the sofa, tapping away on a laptop.

He turns his gaze to us, and I'm met with the greenest eyes—ones I saw last night at dinner. They're almost luminous in the low light of the room. He's dressed in a white T-shirt, a dark pair of jeans, and Chucks. He's the complete opposite of Ash. His arms are inked, and I wonder if he has space for more. There are patterns and images all over his forearms, right up to his wrists. I didn't see them last night, because he had a long-sleeved shirt on.

"Hello again." He smiles, and my breath catches in

my throat. He's handsome. No. He's more than that—he's beautiful, exquisite. His dark hair falls across one eye, looking as messy as Ash's, and I glance behind me, gazing into the blue depths.

When I glance over at the other man again, I smile and offer him a greeting. "Ember?" My voice comes out shy, a whisper, but he heard it because he gifts me another grin that only causes my cheeks to burn and I realize they're probably bright red.

How are both of these men so gorgeous? It should be illegal to look this good.

"This is my brother," Ash tells me. "As I understand it, you've met already and shared dinner." The smooth tone comes from behind me, and my heart is hammering loudly in my ears. They are brothers. That's why Ember was so familiar.

"But . . ." I turn to Ember. "I don't understand."

He smiles, rising from where he's sitting before setting the laptop on the table and making his way over to us, stopping mere inches from me. "I wanted to see you again, princess." His voice is like rich, warm chocolate, with a hint of spice. There's a huskiness to it I recall from last night that causes goosebumps to rise on every inch of my skin.

"And I told him that you'd be here with me this evening," Ash fills in his body against mine, cocooning me in his warmth. He's taller than me, so when he dips his head, allowing his mouth to whisper along my bare shoulder, I shiver in response. "There are rules in this bedroom, Kitten," he murmurs. "If you don't want something to happen, it won't. Please don't be afraid of us."

"I'm not afraid," I bite out confidently, attempting to hide my trembling. But panic is slowly twisting in my gut. *Would they hurt me?* I turn to Ash, then to Ember, and weigh up my options. I could probably fight one off, *but both?* I don't stand a chance. They're playing a game, toying with me, and I struggle with the anxiety gnawing in my gut.

I meet a green gaze and offer a shaky smile. "It's nice to see you again, Ember," I tell him.

"Shall I call you Flame, or do you prefer Katerina?" he asks, lifting my hand before he presses a kiss to my knuckles, eliciting another soft shiver that travels over my form.

"Since you already know my name, call me Kat."

He nods with a smile, one that shows off his dimples, and I realize now how much he looks like Ash. And Ember's words come back to me suddenly. *My brother is the eldest by about . . . Two minutes.* Twins. Not identical, but at a push, they definitely could pass for each other.

"Kitten, why don't you have a seat? I'll grab us some drinks," Ash says, as he steps around me. He shrugs off his jacket and hangs it over the back of one of the wingback chairs. Then he unbuttons his cuffs, and I can't drag my eyes away as he rolls his sleeves up to his elbows. His skin is tanned, just like his brother's, but there are no tattoos in sight. Where one brother is an inked canvas, the other is bare of any marks, but even so, both are beautiful to look at. Just what have I gotten myself into?

"So, why did you want to see me again?" I question Ember, meeting his inquisitive gaze as we settle on the sofa. His green eyes shimmer with mischief, a look that matches his brother's.

"Call me curious," he says confidently, leaning back against the cushions. Even though he's dressed casually, there's something almost regal about him. He sits as if he's been trained to be upright at all times, rigid and poised. Come to think of it, both brothers are alike in that way as well.

Ash sets down three glasses filled with red wine. He lifts one, offering it to me, and the other to his brother. He takes the last glass and says, "To an evening of intrigue."

His toast gives me pause, and I wait for them both to sip at their drinks before I do the same.

I meet blue eyes, watching Ash for a moment before I voice the question that's been sitting on the tip of my tongue for a while. "Ash, what's going on?"

"Tell us about you?" Ember says, responding before his brother can say anything more. He seems enamored with me, not offering his brother a glance.

I cast my gaze toward the man beside me on the sofa, and question, "What do you want to know that you don't already?"

"I have an offer I'd like to make you, Katerina. But first, I'd like to get to know the girl that's stepped into this room." He waves his hand in the air, gesturing toward the door.

"Well, like I told you last night, I want to study, majoring in music. Make my parents proud. I lost them at a young age. My focus is a career and to get out of this *job* I'm doing," I respond before taking a big gulp of wine, hoping it will calm my nerves and allow me to relax somewhat. "I want to have a normal life."

"And you had mentioned to Ember and me that you'd grab any opportunity to do so?" Ash asks, watching me with a stare that burns right through me. It's as if he's attempting to set me on fire with a glance.

"Yes, I did say that. And I would. My education has always been important to me, and I just want to do the one thing I know my mother and father would've wanted for me if they were still alive," I confess. They could help, but I can't come right out and ask. Nerves have set in, and my heart is thudding wildly at the notion that they could offer me something I need.

I set my glass on the table, wanting to keep a clear head because I'm not sure where they're heading with this conversation. And if it's something I'm not prepared for, I need to be able to fight back.

I'm wary of anything that comes my way that seems far too perfect, too good to be true because it usually is. Everything comes at a price. Every silver lining has a dark storm cloud hovering close by.

"Ash and I have a proposition for you," Ember tells me, his gaze casting over me with nothing but friendliness and affection. They're not here to hurt me, and it shows in his honest expression. He turns his attention to his brother before he lands those deep green eyes on me once more. "We'd like to assist you, pay your tuition without you having to repay us, and—"

"Oh, no." I stand up, setting the glass on the table. "I

can't—"

"Sit." Ash's commanding tone is icy when he bites out the word, causing me to flinch. I glance at him, finding his cold azure eyes watching me intently. "Please." He tacks on afterward softening his command, appearing to notice my unease.

I don't obey him—not this time. Instead, I pin him with a stubborn glare, crossing my arms in front of my chest. "I'm not a charity case." Even though I do need help, I have to be able to repay them. Somehow.

He arches a brow at me, and I can tell he's not happy with this turn of events. But I'm more nervous than I'm letting on. If they think I'll be shared between them for a chance at school, they're wrong. Yes, this *job* may not be perfect, but it's the easiest thing I can do to get myself out of the hole I've been in, but I won't be a puppet for them to use.

"You came to this room to get fucked," Ash grits out through clenched teeth, and I wonder where his anger is coming from. "If that's how you want to do this, I can certainly assist you, Kitten," he tells me with a smirk. The corner of his mouth tilts into that wolfish grin and my stomach flutters with lively hummingbirds.

My hands are trembling when I think about him

taking me. "I was . . . I mean I . . . There's just . . ."

"Please." This time it's Ember who implores me. "Just listen to our proposition." He sounds so earnest; I struggle to deny him.

"I'm not looking for handouts, Ember. As much as I—"

"Katerina." Ember's voice caresses my name, calming me somewhat.

I'm still confused how two men, young enough to be at college themselves, can even afford this hotel, the drinks, the clothes, let alone offering to pay for some girl they hardly know to attend college?

As much as I want to refuse and walk out, I can't deny the pull I feel toward them both. Not just a physical pull but an emotional one.

I nod and find myself saying, "I'm listening."

I'm not sure why, but I want to hear what they have to say. If it has any bearing on my future, perhaps I'll be able to consider it. It's been so long since I've been given a reason to hope and maybe this will come to fruition.

If I tell them no and leave right now, I'll regret not hearing them out. I can always do that before refusing their offer. Maybe, just maybe, I could have a chance at a life outside of this. At least, that's what I hope they're proposing.

"Since my brother is in charge of the finances"—Ash waves his hand in the air toward Ember, who's smiling as he watches us intently— "he'll give you the contract with the terms and conditions."

"Just ignore Ash and his snark." Ember winks, patting me on the arm affectionately. They're both so different, so beautiful in their own flaw-filled way.

"I am." I smile, and his responding chuckle only makes the butterflies in my belly come alive. He's the gentle one. There's something almost tender about how he regards me that makes me feel at ease. But it's Ash who sparks a fire in my stomach, one that seems to burn me from the inside out each time I'm near him. *Focus, Kat. Listen to what Ember has to say. Look at him, stop thinking about Ash.*

"The documents in this folder stipulate your contract, set out for the next four years. You will be our ward, for lack of a better word, and we'll be the benefactors of your studies." His explanation causes me to still once I pick up the paperwork.

"Benefactors?"

"We'll pay for you to study, but . . ." His words taper off.

I hold my breath as if a flame is dancing along with

my heart, waiting for it to be blown out by a gust of wind. This has to be some kind of joke, but he doesn't offer a punchline.

Ember's scorching gaze turns to Ash who's regarding us closely, his stare boring into me. "We need your agreement that you'll allow us to be your guardians, so you would have to sign a contract," Ember finally offers.

"What? I don't understand. I'm nobody to you both. Why would you want to do this for a stranger?"

"We'd like to offer you a place to stay. If you're not working for Maria, she may not want you to live in the house you're in at the moment."

"You want me to live with you?" I sound incredulous. I'm confused as to how this is even real life right now. A chance to study is one thing, but to move in with them is taking it one step too far. "I—I . . . This is extreme. What if I want to keep my job?"

"You won't." Ash's voice is heated, commanding, causing me to look at him. His face is rigid, his jaw ticking, and I wonder if it's perhaps jealousy that's turning him to stone right before my eyes.

"If you decide to take us up on the offer and keep your job, we understand," Ember tells me slowly. But I know he's trying to placate his brother and me.

"It's one or the other," Ash says then, his tone hard and unyielding. "No ward of mine will be whoring herself out."

I wince at his harsh words.

"If you do live with us, it would be nice to offer you extra tutoring if you wish. Perhaps you'd want to major in art; I could help you with your projects." Ember says, his smile lighting up his expression.

"I wanted to major in music, but I was leaning toward art as a subject as well." I nod solemnly, and Ember must notice the melancholy in my expression.

"Ash is well versed in music; he's fluent in piano, violin, and the cello. He'll teach you those. I could offer you classes in art. I've been painting since before I was reading." He smiles a smile that could burn out a million stars. "We want you, Katerina, to be ours." His words turn my body fiery hot.

"I just . . . I need time. This is a lot to take in," I tell him.

"Think about the money as a scholarship. If you were offered a full scholarship, you would be at school right now," Ember reasons with me, and I nod because it's true. "So, all that's different here is that you'll have a place to call your own. A home where you're safe and looked after."

"That's what I don't understand. You don't know

me." They're offering me a dream come true, but there's always a catch. They've played their cards well. Now it's my turn.

I glance at the paperwork which I need to read through. I don't have a lawyer to help make sense of everything, and I know this isn't something I can enter into lightly.

Even with the dangling carrot of having four years of schooling paid for, to up and move into a house with two men who are practically strangers, is another thing entirely.

"Let me understand this correctly; I get the money, the scholarship, but I also get a place to stay?" I question, perching on the edge of the sofa. I'm nervous, shaking because I want to say yes, no, and laugh it off as a joke.

Tears prick my eyes when I think about being able to go to school. But I feel like I'm being pranked, and it's not something I can handle right now. Twisting my fingers together, I tremble at the prospect of making such a life-changing decision. I wonder if they can see how nervous I am.

"You put me up for the duration of this contract? This sounds . . . I mean, this is . . . It's a . . ."

"Business transaction." Ash's voice comes out cool

and calm. He's not frazzled in any way, and I wish I could be like that.

"Why would you do this? I don't understand?" I question, my glance flitting between both brothers. A set of green and a pair of blue eyes meet mine, but the brothers don't respond. "I'll need to read over the contract and let you know. If, and I mean if, I agree then I want to make sure you both know if I sense anything amiss, I'll walk out. If I feel uncomfortable, or if something is not what we agreed upon, I leave. No questions asked, and I still get my scholarship."

"You drive a hard fucking bargain, Kitten," Ash smirks, using the nickname he's gifted me. He's the asshole of the two, and if it weren't for him, I would never have set the bar so high. But I have a feeling, he'd be the one to break the agreement. I don't know how or why, but something tells me Ash would be up for playing this far too dirty.

"When my future is on the line. . ." I turn to regard him, ". . . I have to focus. And like I said, this isn't forever." I wave my hand, gesturing to the dress I'm wearing. "I need to go to school to free myself from what I'm doing now, and if you're offering it, I'm willing to take it. And you . . ." I point to Ash. ". . . may try to break me because that's your game, but I'm not easily broken."

The corner of his mouth tilts into a mischievous smirk. "Me? I'll never try to break you, Kitten. I may try to tame you, tamper your heat, but I'll never extinguish your fire. And you know why?" He doesn't wait for me to respond. He continues as he nears me, his body looming over me, and I'm caught in this intensity. "Because I love it when you burn me."

"I need to think about it. I need time."

EMBER

SHE'S PERFECT.

Nothing I'd ever imagined, yet she's everything both Ash and I needed. I want her to say yes, to agree to our terms, but it's been one long night already, and it's not even ten.

"Forty-eight hours." My voice is curt, and she glances at me. "You have until Sunday to decide. If you'd like to come to the house and see what we're offering, you're welcome to. Either Ash or I will collect you," I tell her.

I've never been so nervous to hear someone respond to a proposal. But I understand her hesitancy. I respect it. She's looking out for herself and being responsible like she told me at dinner. However, there's no way she can refuse because this is everything she's wanted. Then again, to give up her freedom and move into our home when she doesn't know us—not as well as we know her—I get it.

She's got a good head on her shoulders.

I smile.

"I'll look through it over the next couple of days," she tells me.

God, I've never been this close to a woman who makes me want to fuck her violently and take care of her in the same breath. My brother has just poured himself a whiskey, and I know by the time the night is through, he'll have gone through a bottle. Perhaps he's as nervous as I am. One thing I've noticed is that he's enamored by her.

My plan will work perfectly. I just need to toy with my brother to get him fired up, and this will be easy. Everything will fall into place.

"Will you tell me why you're doing this?" she finally asks. Her voice is a whisper, raspy, and filled with apprehension, but I have a feeling her intrigue will keep her in our midst.

"I run my father's company," Ash starts with an explanation. "We offer scholarships to students who we deem need assistance."

"And you offer them a place to stay as well?" She challenges, causing me to chuckle. Their chemistry is remarkable, and watching them like this gives me peace that she'll be good for Ash.

I wonder if he'll ever fall for her entirely. *Would he change his ways to make her happy?* I've never known him to care for any of the women he's bedded. He may be friendly to them, strangers mostly because my brother isn't someone who finds himself in relationships, which makes me wonder if she'll get under his skin.

I hope she does.

"No, not at all. But after learning about you, we thought you may enjoy having a semi-permanent home, rather than that shared house," Ash tells her. "If you live at Addington Hall, you'll have your own wing to do with as you wish."

She narrows her eyes at him, and I know their playful banter will only bring life to the mansion. "Your last name is Addington?" she questions, stilling my tapping on the laptop.

Ash nods. "Yes."

"Interesting," she says softly as she flicks the pages of the contract, not reading the words, appearing to ponder what she's just learned.

"Why?" he asks her, settling in the wingback chair, watching her intently with those deep blue eyes that are simmering with amusement. He's so calm, and I wonder if she'll put two and two together.

"My lawyer was an Addington." Her observation turns my blood cold. "I was sixteen when my parents died, and he took on my case with another lawyer that fought for me, but they lost to the state in the end." Her words are drenched in sadness, and I wonder just how to answer her.

But Ash takes the lead. "And you remember the man . . . Addington?"

"Yes, he was good to me. He tried so hard. He made his lawyer spend hours looking at my case from every angle, scouring paperwork in the hopes of getting me a good home," she tells us, glancing between us.

It's as if the world tilts on its axis. I school my features and shrug it off. My father was good to her. I want to admit it right there. I want to tell her who we are and why we're really doing this, but Ash's burning glare stops me.

"My uncle is a lawyer, but we haven't seen him in a long time. He doesn't spend time with us and hasn't done since we were much younger. Perhaps he took on the case when he was in the city a few years ago selling his shares in my father's company," he lies, and I turn away, focusing on the screen.

Katerina takes the contract, holding onto it like a lifeline. I know more questions are coming. "Explain more about your father's company and the scholarship options."

She looks at Ash when she asks this.

"My father was a good man and always made sure to do his part in the community. A long time ago, he decided he'd start awarding scholarships to students who showed promise," Ashton speaks. "When I went through the applications, your name was one of the first on the list."

I glance up at this. We both went through the names, and hers wasn't in the submissions we received. Another lie to add to the never-ending pile we've already stocked up against us.

"I don't understand," she utters in shock. The awe in her tone tells me she's picking up on Ash's story, and I hope she doesn't call him out on it.

Ash smirks. "What?"

"I didn't apply for something like this. I never thought about applying for a grant through a company. It felt so far out of reach. I mean, the college has offered me a partial scholarship, perhaps they could've applied for me."

"Maybe," my brother tells her. "Unless the Dean, who was one of my father's best friends figured you had promise and sent through your details."

"Why? What makes me different?" she asks, flitting her gaze between us before continuing, "Surely there are other more deserving students."

"Don't get me wrong, Kitten," Ash smirks. "You're meant to work hard, study, and get your degree." He gulps down his whiskey as I pour myself one.

I told him this wouldn't be as cut and dry as he expected. She's a strong woman, and being on her own for so long, she's clearly grown weary of people. I don't blame her. I would be too if I were in her shoes.

"I'll take this home tonight and think about it." She smiles at me, then pins Ash with a scowl. "If I sign, you're not the one in charge of the paperwork. I want Ember to finalize it. No changes, no sneaky add-ons. And I keep my home for the time being. Giving up the house I've come to know with Isobel isn't something I would consider just yet."

"Like I said, Kitten"—Ash smirks— "you drive a hard bargain."

I settle on the couch, watching them banter. The tension in the room is hanging heavily with lust. We both pin her with heated stares, and I wonder if she'd ever let me, or Ash, touch her, kiss her, or take her and claim her.

She likes him. I notice her blushing cheeks, the way her gaze drifts to him every so often, and I can't help but smile. Let's just hope my brother doesn't fuck this up. Having her in our home may offer me more insight into her and her feelings for him.

Each night Ash has spent with a woman, I've wondered if that will be it. The day he tells me he's in love. My fear isn't losing him to someone else; it's him turning into our father. I've always ensured he remains true to himself, and I wonder what would happen one day if I'm no longer there.

My heart aches at the thought of not being near my brother, of not seeing him prosper and find the happiness he deserves. There's too much of our father in him it scares me at times.

I know I have to leave now. I only came to be here when he gave her the agreement. My work is done. It's so archaic: a contract to provide a girl something she needs. I wish she would just put her trust in us, in this, but she doesn't even know we *have* to give this to her.

"I'll pick you up in the morning," I tell her, "I'm leaving now. I have a few things to do." My words cause her to frown. But I need to get home, or my brother will learn far too much tonight about what I'm hiding.

"Tomorrow?"

"To take you on a tour of the estate and the house. You can have lunch with me, and we can talk more about your options."

"Oh." Her mouth falls open, plump lips forming an O, and my mind wanders somewhere it really shouldn't. *She's not mine. She can't be.*

"Don't be frightened; we won't be alone. There is staff in the house for most of the day, and I'll bring you home when you're ready."

"Thank you, Ember. I look forward to it." This time, she gifts me a smile that grips my heart, and my chest tightens. "I guess I'm just nervous."

Her admission causes me to nod. "I understand, princess."

"Kitten," Ash interrupts. "If we were here to hurt you, you wouldn't be walking out of this room. But then again, I would want to sample those luscious lips, so as long as you never kiss me, you're fine."

"You're such an asshole," I bite out, burning him with a glare.

Kat smiles. "I would have to agree with Ember on that."

"Never once denied it, darling." Ash chuckles, leaving us in the lounge area when he heads into the bedroom. Seconds later, I hear him on the phone, and I realize he must be talking to Josiah—one of the men who work for us at the house.

"Thank you for trying to ease my worry," Kat tells me in a conspiratorial whisper, causing me to laugh out loud.

"I understand why you would be concerned. I would be too," I inform her. "Ashton gets drunk sometimes and says stupid things which frustrate me. You won't be hurt in our care. That I can assure you of."

She offers me a smile. It's sweet and innocent, and it pulls at my soul. She's not ours to take, but we're stealing her anyway. An exquisite rose amongst the flaming thorns. And I know if she ends up staying, she'll only burn and bleed.

But that's all the more reason for us to keep her. To lick her wounds, to heal her pain, and to make sure we're the only ones in the world who can hurt her. Because we can make her whole again. And I plan on doing that and so much more.

"It's done." Ash's voice breaks my train of thought. "Josiah has been instructed to drive you tomorrow," he tells me.

Nodding, I rise. "Thanks. I'm heading home," I inform them.

"Okay, thank you." Kat's voice sounds sad, or disappointed, an emotion I can't quite put my finger on.

Meeting her gaze, I offer a smile. "I'll see you

tomorrow, sweetheart. Be ready at eleven," I confirm. "Ash." I offer my brother a nod. Without waiting, I head out, leaving them to stare at my retreating back.

"I'm sorry, Kat. I'm so fucking sorry." I tell the empty space of the elevator once I'm shut in alone. Guilt sits in my gut like a poison, and I wonder if she'll ever forgive us for this once she learns the truth.

KATERINA

MY BED IS LUMPY WHEN I ROLL ONTO MY BACK. The sun is peeking through the window, but I keep my eyes closed, not wanting to face reality just yet. After Ash brought me home last night, he dropped me off and waited until I was inside before driving away. Once he was gone, I could breathe again.

Even though I was in bed by midnight, my mind ran in circles well into the early hours of this morning. Every negative thought and every positive outcome have flitted through my imagination. I should feel happy, but even with their promise, I feel like something is wrong. As if there's a storm approaching and I'll be among the debris left behind, swished this way and that.

If I sign the contract, I really have no idea what I'm getting myself into. All I do know is I'll be able to go to school. I'm desperate. In times of need, we tend to do stupid things and make rash decisions. And that's why I have to take time today to read through each page and make sure I'm comfortable.

Agreeing to allow them to pay is one thing, but moving into a house with two men who I have only seen on occasion? That's something else entirely.

"Mama, what do I do?"

I've been thinking about how to tell Maria I no longer want to work for her. I gave myself twelve months, and now, after a short time, I have an option to walk away. As much as I want to say yes, I'm also aware that I need to be careful. I grew up too quickly, and even though I'm still a teenager, I'm more aware of the world around me. More so than if I had my parents watching out for me all the time.

I know what Ash and Ember are giving me will secure my future. One that will allow my dreams to come true. For the first time in a long while, there's light at the end of the tunnel. And having a chance at a better life gives me a flicker of hope.

I take a long look around the room. The space and everything in it is merely for convenience. I have no emotional attachment to anything in this bedroom, aside from the box of photos under my bed. They're the only part of my family I have left.

Two years feels like a lifetime without my parents. I try once more to recall my father's laugh, my mother's melodic giggle, but both have faded as if they'd burned to ash along with the store my father put his heart and soul into.

The night two police officers told me the news, I became detached from everything around me. Nothing had prepared me for actually walking up to the site and seeing the destruction the fire left in its path.

The police had ruled it an accident. A gas leak is what they'd said after the investigation. Something that could've been *missed*. The police confirmed the pipe had needed repair.

Even though my father was meticulous in his work and had far too much pride in his store to miss a problem when it cropped up, I later learned he wasn't the man I thought he was.

Tired of rehashing the past, I push off the bed. I slowly pad over to the closet and pull open the doors. I grab my toothbrush, along with my small toiletry bag, and head into the shared bathroom.

After freshening up, I'm in my room pulling on a jumper when Isobel saunters in as she's done so many times before.

"Where are you off to?" Her question stills me, and I meet her curious gaze. When I was lonely, with nowhere to go, she offered me a chance at trying to make it on my own. And now, I'm considering leaving and moving in with Ash and Ember.

Am I? Perhaps, yes. *Would I be able to walk into their house and feel at home?* I don't know.

"I . . ." Unsure of what to tell her, I gift her a smile, a fake one, and tell her a story. "I'm heading out with a friend. I may have a chance of going to school, and he's going to show me around." With every word I utter, the lies burn my tongue, reminding me the more I voice them, the deeper I'm digging into a hole I may not be able to come back from. And the guilt that weighs on me is cumbersome.

"Oh?" Her dark brows furrow. "Just like that?"

Meeting her gaze, I sigh, realizing I have to give her something. Anything. "I am not moving out. I'm still deciding how it's going to work, but he's offering to pay for my studies. I can't deny I'm struggling with everything right now and it seems like a good opportunity. A scholarship. Something I've been praying for since I was a kid." I sit on the bed before reaching for her hand. "It's the first time I feel as if I have a chance at a normal life."

She smiles, squeezing my fingers, and then pulls me into a hug. Her arms wrap around me, and I allow her to hold me. Her affection causes my eyes to burn with emotion forcing me to blink back the tears.

"Okay, as long as you don't make a rash decision. You can stay here as long as you need." She grins. Pulling away and meeting my gaze, Isobel winks. "Tell me, is this friend of yours hot?"

I can't help but laugh at her question. How do I even explain Ember and Ash? They're both perfect, both beautiful, and I realize I don't want to share them with anyone.

"He's . . . I don't know, different." My cheeks heat with embarrassment.

Her gaze narrows with a glare before she responds, "Different? Oh my god, he's not some weirdo who lives in a dungeon or something?"

The giggle that bubbles in my chest tumbles from my lips. I can't deny I'm curious as to what their home looks like. I'm sure it's big—bigger than I'm used to. Excitement slowly trickles through me, knowing that I'm going to be seeing it today.

"Well, I'll let you know," I tell her, "If I do decide to leave, I'll always keep in contact with you. You've been the best friend I've had."

It's not a line to get her off my back; I mean it. I would like to have someone to confide in. Maybe Bel can be my voice of reason. I have a feeling I'll need someone to talk to. I'm out of my depth. I'm caught among Ash and Ember—their charismatic ways, attractive smiles, and intoxicating personalities.

"I'd like that. I haven't really connected with anyone since I've been living here," Isobel confesses in a tone that's filled with so much sadness, it matches my own.

"Listen to me." I lean in, offering her a smile, one that I really feel. It's easy to paste on a fake grin or offer a laugh that's forced, but right now, in this moment, I feel it down to my very soul. "We'll both be okay. I'm always here if you need me."

"Thanks, Kat. I appreciate it." She smiles, leaning back on my bed. "Tell me about your friend. Is he single? Does he have any friends who are looking to meet up?" She laughs.

I'm about to respond when a knock at the door sounds, startling me. I head toward it and pull it open, thinking it's one of the girls, but it's not. The pair of eyes that meet mine is the brightest, most beautiful startling green.

"Ms. Nielsen." He smiles. Ember Addington. "I trust you're well this morning. I'm a little earlier than expected."

"Ember, I . . . I . . . yeah." Cringing at the way I'm bumbling my words, I step back, allowing him to enter the room. It's a mess, and I can't help burning with embarrassment when he steps into the room and leans down to pick up a fluorescent pink bra. I snatch it from his fingers before shoving it into a drawer.

"Hi," Isobel greets and smiles at Ember. He's intoxicating to the point of distraction. "I'm Bel."

"It's lovely to meet you, Bel." Ember grins. Taking her hand, he places a small kiss on her knuckles, as if we've just stepped into the nineteenth century. "I didn't realize Katerina had a friend here."

"Oh, we've known each other for a short time, but she's my girl." Isobel smiles. "And if anything happens to her . . ." The threat she doesn't voice tapers into silence, causing me to cringe inwardly.

"She'll be well taken care of. I give you my word." He offers her one of his signature smirks, that shows off his dimples in each cheek. The same one he gave me the night of our date. He's dangerous, seductive, and charming in one attractive package.

"I'm almost ready," I blurt out.

Ember turns to regard me with a smile. "I can wait. Ash is at the office, so there's no rush. Did you need some . . ." He picks up another bra which is lying on the bed, a black lace one, and smirks at me when my cheeks warm with a blush. ". . . help?"

"No, just grabbing my purse and then we can leave."

"Kat, I'll see you soon." Isobel smiles, pressing a kiss to my cheek. "I'm only a phone call away," she whispers. She doesn't need to finish her promise because it's there. A friendship that I never thought I would have.

Once I'm alone with Ember, he looks over at me. "Don't be scared." Ember winks playfully. "You're safe with us. And today, it's merely a tour of the house. I'll show you where you would be able to set up your own space." There's that affectionate grin again. The one lingering glance that makes my stomach tumble wildly.

"I'm not scared; not right now at least. I think I'm nervous."

"Something tells me you're stronger than both of us put together. If we can assure you of one thing—being in our home would be the same as living here with the girls. With the exception that we're just a little more on the rugged side." He teases, eliciting a laugh from me. The ease with which he consumes my attention lightens the rigidity in my shoulders.

Ember stalks toward me where I'm standing between the boxes and suitcases which I still haven't unpacked. He places his index finger under my chin, tipping my head backward. Green eyes pierce me, holding me hostage, and my breath catches in my throat. My heartbeat is wild and erratic, slamming against my ribs. "How about you trust me?"

I can't help a smile tilting my lips before responding easily, "Trust is something that's earned."

He tips his head to the side as if considering my response with a grin on his face and I know if I'd said that to Ash, the reaction would be so different. He finally nods. "True. But we're giving you a dream. How about the benefit of the doubt?" he counters with a smirk.

"You have that for now. I've agreed to go to your house today. Haven't I?"

"Good girl." He smiles, and I can't move. Not right now while he's pinning me with a gaze so intense, so arresting, that I'm unable to formulate a proper comeback.

That makes me wonder if I'll ever be able to say no to Ash, Ember, or their offer.

KATERINA

THE CAR PULLS UP A LONG DRIVE, AND I'M IN AWE of the house before us. Two floors of open brick reach toward the sky. There's a wraparound balcony on the second floor which is made of white metal. At least, that's what it looks like from here. "This is amazing," I tell Ember, who's smiling beside me.

"Let's go inside. I promise it only gets better." He offers me a hand, and we exit the vehicle. The driver disappears toward the garage, and soon, Ember is escorting me to the house, which is even more breathtaking inside.

The entrance foyer is vast with white marble tiles. Paintings hang along the walls, which I pause to take in with awe. I'm sure they're more expensive than anything my parents ever had, probably even more than the entire house I grew up in.

"Let me show you the living spaces," Ember offers

with a grin, tugging me along behind him. My gaze can't flit fast enough to take everything in. The white tiles follow us through to the kitchen where everything is ceramic, steel, and marble.

"I've never been in such an opulent place before."

"There's more." He winks, and I follow him through to the living room which has floor-to-ceiling windows that overlook the back garden. The furniture is older here, more for comfort than luxury. Dark leather, with hundreds of cushions in either corner. There are three sofas, one wingback chair, and a fireplace which holds photos on the mantle, along with a painting of what looks like the garden just on the other side of the windows hanging on the wall.

There's a dark carpet under a glass coffee table, and it momentarily takes me back to my old living room and the table my mother was so proud of. Instantly, my heart aches, and I'm blinking back tears.

"Hey." Ember rushes to me, and his hands grip my shoulders, his green eyes peeking into my gray ones. "I didn't mean to upset you."

"It's okay, just . . . sometimes my memories are more painful than I care to admit." My honesty has him nodding.

"Yes, I know that far too well," Ember tells me forlornly, and I wonder if he's talking about losing his parents. "Let's go upstairs. I can show you what would be your bedroom if you decided to move in."

He looks so excited, and I don't want to deny him. The sun streams through the windows on the south side of the house, and I can imagine basking in the warmth here on a sunny afternoon while getting lost in a book.

When we climb the staircase, I can't help but gasp at the amount of art on the walls. Every panel is filled with an exquisite piece. The carpet is soft underfoot, and our steps are silent as we make our way down the hall.

"This is the west wing; Ash is on the east along with me. You'll have this section to yourself, so you'll have more space than in your current house," he explains as he pushes open a door and allows me to step inside. "This will be yours."

My bedroom.

It's decked in white and soft cream, deep burnt orange, and dark red. There are dark roses on the curtains, almost as if the petals had been burned. Along with the white furniture, the contrast of colors makes the space breathtaking. With a window seat which overlooks the forest behind the mansion and a large swimming pool, I can't help but wonder what I did to deserve this.

It's beautiful and different, and it fits me more than

they both know.

"This is incredible, Ember," I tell him.

"But?" Mischief dances in his expression.

I settle on the window seat, my mind still racing in a few hundred different directions. I meet his inquisitive gaze. "I can't move into your home when I barely know you both," I tell him. "Like I said, I've been taught to trust only when it's earned, and right now, I'm more wary about why I'm your pet project."

"Fair enough." He grins. "For a long time, I've stayed alone in this house. Ash would be out at the hotel, and I'd be here, with my paintings." Ember sits on the mattress, not too far from me, but he offers enough space to make me feel less nervous. There's a sadness in his tone, and I wonder what's brought it on.

Tipping my head to the side, I regard him. "You don't have a girlfriend?"

He shakes his head. "Never wanted one. If I wanted a release, I'd pay for it, and move on. I'm not made to love someone, Kat."

Shock lances my chest, "What? Why? Anyone can love, and you've certainly showed you care for people." I don't know why I feel utter devastation, for someone to not have any inkling for love or a relationship causes me to wonder what happened to him.

He sighs, scrubbing his hand over his jaw while keeping his eyes on the carpet he answers. "My focus is always my brother. He's so broken, at times I wonder if he'll turn into my father." Ember glances at me and says, "I want him to have a forever. I don't have that option. Not right now."

My brows furrow. It sounds like he's speaking in riddles. It doesn't make sense to me that he wouldn't be able to find someone who loves him. "I don't understand."

"I can't explain it, Kat. Just allow me this, please," he pleads with fervor.

"Okay." I offer him a sad smile before asking, "Tell me about Ash?"

His eyes narrow on me, and I realize I've given away my interest. Perhaps it wasn't very subtle, but I do want to get to know Ash better. He's intriguing. Mystery cloaks him, and I can't deny I'd like to uncover it.

"My brother is . . . hard work."

"I don't doubt that." I smile, and for the first time since I walked into the house, I feel at ease. Like I belong here.

"Why don't we make lunch, and I'll tell you whatever you'd like to know?" He rises, gesturing with his head for me to follow, and I do.

In the kitchen, Ember places ingredients on the island in the center of the room and tells me to sit on the stool. "Would you like to make cookies while I make us some sandwiches?"

Nodding, I tell him, "I used to love baking with my mother." While I open the containers and packets of ingredients, I question, "So, tell me about you, before we get to Ash."

"Well, I grew up with a twin brother, as you know. We loved pranking each other as kids. But as we got older, Ash was always irresponsible in his choices, and there were so many times I wondered if he'd ever want to take over the company."

"Why did he?"

Ember glances my way. "Because he was the better choice." The mischievous smile that adorns his handsome face makes him seem younger than I know he is. With a wink, he adds, "he will always be a better choice." His comment tells me he's no longer just talking about the company.

"What about you?" I change direction.

He smiles, wistfully. Something is hiding behind those green eyes, and I find myself curious as to what it could possibly be. Ember is like a flame, and I'm a moth, wanting to get closer, to learn who he is. But as much as I want to fly toward the light, Ash makes me burn from the inside. Vastly different emotions, from two very different men.

"I'm not a leader. I prefer to be behind the scenes."

"Any past relationships? Ever wanted to be more like your brother?" My questions tumble freely, I shouldn't be so forward, but I can't stop myself.

He laughs out loud at my question. "You're really going in for the kill there. I've never wanted a relationship. My father taught us business comes first, but deep down, I don't want to leave my brother. I think if I weren't around, he'd fall into the darkness same as my father after my mother died." He shakes his head, his expression turning sad.

As I mix the ingredients in the large bowl he's set out, my stomach tumbles and the scent of the sugary sweetness makes me feel nauseous.

Ember lifts his gaze toward mine and shrugs, "I didn't mean to offload all that on you. I'm sorry."

"No, I mean, I asked. And I'm sorry that you've dealt with so much pain," I tell Ember, feeling more and more at ease with him. As if I'm getting to know him on a deeper level and that calms me. But, as comfortable as he makes me, I notice there isn't a spark between us like there is with Ash.

"Don't be. You should feel comfortable with me, and I want to make sure you do." Ember sets down the plates and watches me for a moment before saying, "We really do just want you to feel as if you belong here. Because you do."

"Thank you. It means a lot to me." The comfortable conversation continues about art and Ember's love of the craft, and I smile as I continue with my task.

And I consider moving into this house.

Having them care for me.

But there's a niggling in my gut that tells me to be careful.

ASH

NOT EVEN TWENTY-FOUR HOURS HAVE PASSED since we gave her the agreement, and I can't get her off my mind. The tension of waiting has got me on tenterhooks. I'm not by any means a patient person—that's my brother—but I know I can't force her hand.

I've also never been so enamored, and I know Ember has noticed it. I realize she's with him right now and I'm not sure if that makes me more tense or calms me somewhat. She's inside the mansion where all our secrets are hidden.

Will she find them? If she does, will she run? Is forgiveness something she'll gift us? Or will the kitten's curiosity take hold and see her agree to our terms?

"Mr. Addington." Frederik saunters into the office as if he owns the fucking place. He knows he doesn't, and I believe he'll soon see I'm the one in charge. "The meeting with Fletcher and Sons is tomorrow," he tells me. "I'll gladly sit in—"

"You're no longer needed to run this meeting," I tell him, shrugging on my jacket. "I'll be taking it, and you will hear about the progress when I officially address the board in a month."

Meeting his gaze, I can't help but smile at the floundering idiot, and I don't deal well with two-faced assholes. He stares at me for a moment, his mouth agape, and I want to laugh. But I shake my head in disappointment.

"Firstly, I've told you before, my father gave *me* the company. You may not believe I'm able to run it, but he did. And there's one other thing I will tell you for free." I lean in, closing the distance between us. "I won't step down just because you think I should."

"It's been a long while since your father died," he utters in a tone that makes my body rigid with anger. A smile lights up his old, wrinkled face which annoys me. As much as I loved our old man, there were many secrets he kept from us. And Ember doesn't know what our dad hid away to ensure we'd love him unconditionally.

Sadly, the moment I walked into the office and I found his safe, I was in for a rude awakening. All those documents he secured behind a heavy metal door glared at me, and I knew there was no other choice. I had to be the one to take over. Once my father's will had been read out, I knew he'd planned it. He knew I was the only one who could learn the truth and not hate him.

Ember being as empathetic as he is would never be able to forgive our dad for what he'd done in the past. He needs love and support, and to believe that Leonard Addington was a saint. All this time, I've hidden the truth to keep him safe, and I'll do it till my dying day.

"That's all for today, Frederik," I tell the old man. "I'll see you tomorrow."

He turns away, heading for the door. He's about to step out of my office, but he stops and holds the door handle. "Your father was always keeping secrets," he utters. "Let's hope you don't do the same. They're vicious things; they poison even the most innocent of flowers."

He's gone a moment later, and I don't even try to unravel what he meant because that's the thing about Frederik—he may have been my father's friend for years, but he's also the most secretive employee in this place. Hiding the Addington secrets has been his number-one goal, and he's undoubtedly accomplished it to date.

Sighing, I settle back in my chair before pulling out my cell phone. Tapping dial on the number, I then hold the device to my ear. When I hear Ember's rushed tone, I wonder just what he's doing.

"What's wrong?"

He chuckles. "Nothing. Kat and I are doing what you, and I used to do as kids," he murmurs in my ear, and my mind starts whirling a thousand miles a minute.

"What do you mean?" I bite out without meaning to.

"Oh, she's attempting to slide down the staircase balustrade. Of course, I had to teach her." Ember's voice is light, carefree, and my heart lurches for a moment.

It's been such a long time since my brother has been happy that it's rather frightening. Well . . . more like frustrating because I want to be with her, to teach her things she doesn't know. And I realize amid my jealousy, it's Ember who needs her most. He's been my support all our lives, never having a girlfriend or other friends outside of our circle, perhaps having Kat there will take away some of the loneliness he must feel.

"Enjoy it. I'll be home in an hour," I tell him finally.

"Oh, that's still a long while," he informs me.

A soft giggle filters over the line and my heart aches. I have to be stronger than this. I should've just let them be, but the masochist in me wouldn't allow it. I want Kat. More than I thought possible. "Yes. There are a few things left to tie up, nothing major. Tell the kitten I'll be home soon" I hang up before my brother can tell me more about how sweet she is.

He didn't want me to make contact with Katerina; he was angry I did. Now, he's the one playing children's games with her while I run our father's company.

I put all my focus into the emails that need my attention and attempt not to think of home. Deep down, all I see is her. With every letter I type and email I send, it's Kat who grips me more than anyone ever has, and I wonder just what I'm going to do the moment she realizes why I'm in her life.

When I glance at the time, I notice I need to leave. I promised Ember an hour. It's time to go home and face her once more. I'm certain she would've agreed to dinner with us. I wish she'd just move in so I can keep an eye on her.

Sighing, I rise from my seat, wondering what I'm going to find when I walk into the house. To see her in the space, she should never have entered.

Our plan was simple—get the girl, fulfill our father's wishes, and ensure that her life is filled with goodness.

Four years.

It's a long time to promise something to someone. To

take time out of your normal life and ensure they're the one who receives your focus. However, I know if anyone can fulfill his promise, it's Ember.

Me?

I'm not so sure.

I sigh before shoving my phone into my jacket pocket, grabbing my keys, and stalking out of the office. The moment I hit the garage, and I slide into my Maserati, I feel my blood begin to simmer. The tension in my muscles only makes my body ache in places I shouldn't be aching; not for her. As I fly down the streets, I keep my mind focused on the road, rather than Katerina Nielsen.

The Bluetooth system in the car rings violently through the speakers. Tapping the button, I wait for my brother to say something.

"Are you on your way home?"

"Yeah," I answer. My voice is tight with anxiety, and I know my twin brother will be able to hear it, and he'll read into it.

"Dinner is almost ready. How far away are you?"

"Pulling up to the gates," I tell him as the wrought iron slides open, scraping along the gravel. "Is there something wrong?"

"No, nothing at all." He hangs up before either of us

can say anything more.

I'm surprised by her allure. I have a feeling Ember is as well. After last night, I noticed his smile when she glanced at him. His affection toward her makes me confident my brother will enjoy having someone around while I'm attending company meetings.

Once I've parked the car, I exit the vehicle and enter through the front door. As soon as I step into the foyer, I'm assaulted by the scent of food. Spices whirl around me, reminding me that we have a guest.

Ember hasn't cooked in years. We have staff for that. But I know how much he loves creating dishes for us to feast on with a lovely glass of wine to accompany the meal. I can't help but sigh when I head into the kitchen to find Kat sitting on the stool at the kitchen counter. She's pressing something I can't see at first, but when she shifts, I notice they're cookies.

"Ash," she breathes, her stormy gaze meeting mine as her eyes widen, and her mouth pops into an O that makes more than just my heart thud.

My zipper feels much tighter than it was seconds ago. The spicy scent of cinnamon and sweet fragrance of sugar wrap themselves around me like a blanket when I reach her.

"How was your day?" Her question is genuine.

I've not had someone ask me that in so long, I'm unsure of what to say to her.

I had meetings.

I thought about her all day.

And I've been stressed wondering just what she'll find if she were to wander through the house.

"Busy," I tell her, allowing my gaze to drift over her body, noting she's wearing a pair of shorts that should be illegal. She's also dressed in a tank top that makes my cock harden considerably, reminding me of how long it's been since I fucked someone. I haven't had anyone in my bed for almost a month now. She's been my focus.

"Oh, okay." She seems disappointed at my response, and I realize she was trying to start a conversation, which I inadvertently knocked down. "We're making dinner," she informs me shyly as if I can't see.

"Yeah, I figured from the smells wafting through the house," I respond. Rounding her, I head farther into the kitchen where I find Ember watching me with a pointed glare. I know I'm an asshole, but this is our game. We play good cop, bad cop all the time.

"I didn't think work was *that* much of a sore subject," he tells me icily. The temperature in the room turns almost

168

arctic, but when Kat shifts on the stool between us, I can't stop my eyes drifting toward her.

She's so focused on her little kitten cookies that she doesn't notice the tension between us. Either that, or she's ignoring us. Perhaps she's not allowing herself to be pulled into the force that is the Addington twins.

"I'm going upstairs," I inform them before heading out of the room.

A soft giggle follows me as I reach the second floor where our bedrooms are situated, and then I hear it—Ember laughing. It's been years since I've heard that sound, and it only serves to frustrate me more.

I shouldn't be jealous. This was our agreement—what we both decided to do. *But why is it I feel like a man scorned by a lover?*

She's not mine.

Ember is my brother.

Even though this isn't going to be forever, I wonder deep down if I'm going to be able to live a lie for the time that we have left.

KATERINA

THE AIR WAS THICK WITH TENSION FROM THE moment Ash walked into the kitchen to when he stalked out. He's a force to be reckoned with, and I'm curious to find out if I would ever survive him. There's a heaviness when both men are in the room, and it makes me wonder just what lies between them. Instead of getting in the middle of it, I tell myself to focus on my own problems.

Tomorrow I have an interview with the Dean, and he'll let me know if I'm able to join classes, those are the only things that I will allow to fill my mind. I plan to sign the agreement tonight. I want to accept their generous gift, as long as I can stay at the house with Isobel. I'll go to school and hopefully be able to pay them back soon.

"Are you sure I'm not imposing?" I question, licking the dough from the spoon which is sticky and sweet. Ember's gaze lands on my lips. He watches me closely as I continue enjoying the sugary goodness.

"Why would you ask that?" he questions, but he's distracted. His heated gaze trails over my lips and fingers, and then meets my own watchful stare.

Shrugging, I set the utensil in the bowl before I respond. "It seems Ash doesn't want me in the house."

"He's always like that," Ember tells me with a rueful smile. "He has a lot of stress at work, and when he's been in meetings most of the day, he becomes . . ."

"An asshole?" I finish his sentence, causing him to smile. A gentle chuckle rumbles through his chest. "I mean, I've only been around him a couple of times, but . . . I don't know, he seems . . ."

"Angry?"

I nod. Ember would know his brother better than I do. But he's right; Ash radiates heated emotions that cause me to wonder what he's really like deep down. I feel like he hides so much more than he shares. Then again, it's only been a week since I first met him.

"My brother has spent his life being angry," Ember tells me almost wistfully. He clears his throat, meeting my inquisitive gaze. "I don't mean . . . I think he has a lot that bothers him. About my father, me, our mother," he continues when I don't respond. "We haven't had it easy, no matter what this looks like." He waves his hand around the huge kitchen that's filled with silver appliances that all look brand new. The tiles look expensive, and I can only guess they're of the finest quality marble, along with the garden that stretches outside for miles.

"Maybe I can talk to him?"

"If I thought that would work, I'd agree. But . . ."

I offer a small smile, realizing my mistake. *Who am I to offer something like that?* I'm only a girl they're giving charity to. A pity gift that allows them to feel less guilty for having so much money. Ash said it himself; their father set up the scholarship program to give back.

I know we're not friends or a couple. It's almost like I'm only here because they feel sorry for me. Not because I mean something to them. My emotions have taken over like they always do, and sadness grips my chest. The coldness holds me, and I know it will never truly be gone. *How can I ever be happy when I'm still so broken and tortured inside?*

"Look, I'm wondering if this was a good idea," I finally utter, toying with the cookie cutter that's lying on the counter top. "Perhaps you can have the driver drop me home?"

Ember stills. He's frozen to the spot when his green

gaze meets mine. There are so many emotions flickering within the depths that they remind me of rustling leaves in a warm summer breeze. When he looks at me, I feel it right down to my soul. The difference between him and Ash is that one offers me warmth, where the other chills me.

It doesn't matter which way I turn. I'm not sure how to trust either of them just yet. I've spent today getting to know Ember, but I still don't really know Ash. And if I'm about to allow them to pay for my schooling, I'll need time to learn who they are.

"We want you here. Not because we feel sorry for you, but because you're . . . you're special to us." Ember's insistence doesn't sell me on the fact that I'm not some charity case to them. I want to do this, to believe it's for my benefit, but there's still a niggling feeling that eats away at me.

Shaking my head, I regard Ember before responding, "You don't even know me."

"We know enough about you to want you here, sweetheart. This isn't a game; it's something we spoke about, and allowing someone to have the future they were meant to means a lot to us, Kat." Ember smiles, holding me hostage with a glimpse at those dimples that slowly peek out.

He closes the distance between us, his mere presence warming me up. He reaches for my face, cupping my cheeks, and holding me so I can't turn away.

"But we also want to know you." His words are whispered, a promise, a balm that calms my erratic heartbeat. "*I* want to know you," he tells me earnestly, and I swear there's an electric current coursing through me in response.

"I'm not going to be a toy for you and Ash to fight over," I tell him, my voice already wavering as the heat of him holds me hostage. I press my palms against his chest, keeping him at a distance. "I don't . . . It's not who I am."

"I know." He lowers his head as if he's embarrassed. But when he lifts his gaze to mine, he tells me, "You're intoxicating. What if you could have us both? Even for a short time?"

"Ember," his name is a whisper, and I know I can't be with him. He's not the one that makes my heart flutter, and I attempt to step back, but I'm stuck between him and the counter.

"You're so beautiful." He leans in, the warmth of his breath fanning over my cheeks when his lips feather along my skin. I shiver in anticipation, as my eyes flutter closed, my lips part on a moan that falls unbidden from my mouth.

"I . . ." Ember's voice is raspy when he finally swallows my objection. His tongue sweeps along mine as it duels for dominance. His lips are hot, molding to my mouth, and I can't stop myself from twining my hands around his neck. I feel drunk, high on his nearness, and I forget where I am, who I am, just for a minute.

His body presses mine to the countertop. I feel every hard ridge of him, from his shoulders to his arms, to the taut hips that taper into a waistline most men would kill for.

His thigh pushes between mine as our kiss intensifies, and it feels like there's a fire burning inside me. It's as if he's lit a match and dropped it on the coals, igniting me from the top of my head to my toes.

I push against Ember, my hands flat on his chest as he steps back, staring at me. "I can't," I tell him. The confusion that swirls in my mind is nothing compared to what's in my chest. Just a couple of days and I'm here, torn between two men. But it's not Ember who's burrowing into my heart; it's his brother.

His gaze penetrates mine. He can see it. A small smile plays on his lips, and he offers a curt nod.

It's Ash. It will always be Ash.

"I'm happy," he tells me and presses a chaste kiss to my cheek.

"Am I interrupting?" Ash's voice cuts through the air, causing Ember to move farther away from me, but he doesn't seem perturbed that his brother is there.

"You are." Ember chuckles.

"I . . . I'm going to freshen up," I mumble in embarrassment. But before I have time to push past Ash at the doorway, his hand shoots out, gripping my arm.

Snapping my gaze to his, I find those beautiful orbs pinned on me. The corner of his mouth kicks into a grin. "The next time you decide to partake in stuff like that, I'd prefer you two take it upstairs. I'm not in the habit of watching my brother hump a girl on the kitchen counter."

He releases me and saunters into the kitchen, leaving me in shock, staring at his back as he opens the fridge and grabs a bottle of beer. As soon as I reach the bathroom on the first floor, I shove the door closed and lean against it, trying to calm my erratic heartbeat. *What are you doing, Kat?*

As much as I'd like to believe in all this, something still niggles at me. *What do they really want?* Being charitable to someone less fortunate is one thing, but I don't think what they're offering me is merely out of the goodness of their hearts.

Lifting my fingers to my lips, I touch them tentatively. The buzz from Ember's kiss still tingles over my mouth, and I wonder how he can be warm like fire, burning me, while Ash is cool and so aloof.

Pulling open the drawers, I check each one, finding them empty. I close the lid of the toilet and sit on the white porcelain. Sighing, I take in the immaculate bathroom. Expensive tiles, glass, and chrome, with towels the color of oranges decking out the space.

The bathtub looks like it could hold a football team. The shower is no different, with two showerheads and a glass wall. In the top drawer of the cabinet is a hair-dryer, along with a straightener. Brand new toothbrushes, toothpaste, and toiletries are all set out as if my hosts were expecting me.

I guess they were.

When I lift my gaze to the mirror, noticing my mouth is slightly swollen from my earlier kiss, my cheeks flushed, and my hair a tangle of chestnut curls.

My reflection is a stranger. She's Katerina, not Flame. For the first time today, I smile at myself and allow happiness into my heart.

But only for a moment.

I've never had opportunities fall into my lap. The past two years have never given me anything that didn't come at a price, and I have a feeling this time is no different. Only, I wish I could figure out what the cost is with the Addington twins.

Tonight, I'll find out why I'm really here.

ASH

"**D**ID YOU ENJOY THAT?"

I swig my beer, keeping my gaze locked on my brother. He doesn't look at me, but I can tell he's pleased with himself. *She's not a toy.* Even as I think it, I know I'm lying to myself. I want to play with her to see how much she can take before she finally breaks.

But Ember? He wants to coax her, to pet and stroke her until she's a docile little kitten in his lap. I'm not a nice man. I never have been. And this time, I'm not going to be anything other than myself.

It's no secret the girl makes my dick hard. She makes me want to do things to her, I've never wanted to do with anyone else. But there's an innocence to her that causes me to want to break her, make her cry and beg, and then slowly put her back together. A puzzle for my personal enjoyment.

179

"As a matter of fact, brother, I did." Ember smiles. His face is lit up with mischief like it always does when he has the upper hand on me. He just doesn't know how much of an advantage he actually has. I want to tell him, but the moment I open my mouth, I shut it again.

"Good," I tell him, attempting nonchalance. "Then you'll enjoy me taking her to the dinner tomorrow night?"

"You mean the black-tie event where you're going to dress her up like Cinderella, and then what?" He crosses his arms in front of his chest, his gaze burning through me, and I can tell he's angry.

"Then you'll be there at midnight, just like we planned," I tell him while shrugging off his hard stare. Ember has always believed people can change, that there's good in everyone. But each time he's given me the benefit of the doubt, I've disappointed him. Not because I want to, but because he loves me too much, and I can't have him doing that.

"So, what? I'm Prince Charming?" He chuckles wryly, shaking his head.

I swallow the rest of my beer before responding, "If that's who you'd like to be, then so be it."

"This isn't a fucking fairytale, Ashton!"

"Calm yourself." I set the bottle on the counter and

head to the fridge to grab another. I know I'm only making him angrier, but I want him to hate me. I want him to remember all our fights when I have to tell him the truth about why I'm doing this.

"Fuck you, brother," he retorts. The words are hissed through his clenched teeth, and I take note of his taut jaw.

"What's wrong?" Kat's sweet voice comes from the doorway, and I watch in awe as my brother visibly calms down with her arrival.

"I was just telling Ember I have something to finish up." I smile, stalking to the doorway where the little kitten is still standing. Her gaze meets mine. The questions that dance in her stormy eyes still me for a moment, and I wonder if I would ever have a chance with a girl like her.

"Are you leaving?" Her voice makes my heart do stupid shit. Things it has no right to do. I should ignore her, walk right by her because she's not here for me. She's here for Ember.

"I have work to do," I tell her with a curt nod.

I take her in for a moment longer, then, without response, offer a nod and turn to walk away. Her burning touch still lingers on my skin, but I can't turn to look at her because I know if I do, I'm breaking every rule I've ever made—don't fall for anyone.

Making my way through the house, I'm still thinking about her as I walk through the dimly lit hallways. I like having her here, there's something calming about it. But Ember's game boiled my blood earlier. Seeing his lips on hers wasn't what I expected to find when I walked into the kitchen. I want to drink, to get obliviously drunk and forget she's in our home, but I know I can't.

I can't forget her.

No matter how I try.

Settling in the chair in my father's office, I close my eyes, not needing to see the dark, dreary antique furniture that still fills this room. When I first walked into the office after his death, I knew I would have my work cut out for me.

Thankfully Ember had no interest in the company. I know why he doesn't want to do it. And the reasons behind his choice make my own heart cave in on itself.

Even though we may disagree on many things, my brother is my life, and I would do anything for him. Seeing him in pain, I feel it down to my core. Our connection as twins has been somewhat supernatural throughout our lives, and now, it's no different. Only this time, he doesn't know what I've done.

The phone echoes shrilly through the room, and

the moment I pick up, I know who it is. "How are you?" I question the man who holds so many lives in the palm of his hand.

"Well, thank you. This girl you've recommended, she is a stellar student," he tells me; something I already know. "I'd love to meet her tomorrow."

"She'll be there as my plus one," I respond easily. "Thank you for taking in the late admission, Dean Waverley."

"Anything for the Addington boys. Your father was a good man."

His words grip my heart, squeezing so tight I'm almost breathless. "We'll see you tomorrow."

He hangs up, and I consider asking him not to mention why I asked him to admit her. It's my last evening with the beauty before I step back and allow my brother to take the lead.

Opening the folder on my computer desktop, I click on the file and scan the agreement. I signed it; Ember did as well. It's not the same one we offered Katerina. She doesn't know what we've planned and as wrong as it is, I know there's no going back now.

Closing the document, I rise from my chair and head to the cabinet against the wall. I pop open the decanter and pour a double shot of amber liquid. My father's favorite became mine when he died. I swallow back the shot before I feel her presence in the office.

"Ash?"

"What are you doing in here?" I grit out, not turning to meet those steel gray eyes. As much as I'd love to cast my gaze on her, I focus on the wall before me. Lowering my head, I pour another shot and pick up the tumbler.

"I . . . I'm not sure what's happened—"

"You should go and eat dinner with Ember," I say, still not looking at her. I know if I do, I'll crumble. I'll feel something when I shouldn't, and that will be a problem. I've watched her for so long it feels as if I know her. But I don't. She's not mine.

"Look, I know you're angry," she says.

"I'm not angry. I just don't need a fucking babysitter," I bite out, spinning on my heel to meet her wide eyes. Her expression tightens with anger.

"You're such a fucking asshole," she spits angrily, and I don't blame her. I don't even tell her she's wrong. She's not.

Shrugging, I settle in the chair and watch her from behind the desk. A classic beauty—her dark, curly hair hangs over her shoulders. Smooth alabaster skin is blemish free, and her pouty lips call to me, making me want to steal them with my own. I can tell she's not wearing a bra and it doesn't help my dick hardening in my slacks.

"I don't know what I did to you—"

"You didn't do shit to me. This is an agreement we're offering you. Like I said, a business transaction. You study, and we pay. That's it," I tell her. "I told you, Kitten, I'm not a nice man, and I hope you don't mistake me offering to pay for your education as an indication that I'll change."

"I don't hold out hope, Ash. It's been a long time since I allowed that emotion to steer me in life. It's a lie. And I don't deal well with lies." Her words ring through me, and I wonder if I should tell her why she's here. Her gaze hardens with anger when I don't make a move to talk to her. Why should I? The only thing I can tell her will hurt her more than anything, so I shrug nonchalantly and sip my drink.

"Then you best leave me to my drink, Kitten," I tell her, flicking my fingers in a gesture of dismissal which I know will annoy her. If this were a world of fairy tales, our princess is nothing short of perfect.

"You really are an asshole, Ashton Addington," she mumbles, her eyes glittering with unshed tears. They look like diamonds under the spotlight—mesmerizing and hypnotic.

"On Saturday, I'd like you to accompany me to a gala event at the university. The dean would like to meet you," I tell her, not bothering to respond to the comment she made.

She crosses her arms in front of her chest, her gaze burning into me. "And what makes you think I'm going to spend the evening with you?"

"Well . . ." I shrug, rising to head back for another refill. "If you don't, the Dean won't meet you, and you'll not be admitted to your course."

"But—"

"Yes or no, Kitten?" The alcohol swishes against the crystal, and I know I've won. She'll soon learn that I always win. There's nothing in this life that I can't get. And Katerina is one of those things.

"Fine. But if you so much as utter a rude word at me once . . ." she informs me, her chin lifting in defiance, and I can't help but chuckle.

She's like a brand new kitten—playful, feisty, and sassy.

I like it.

I like her.

A little too much.

KATERINA

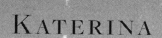

SPINNING ON MY HEEL, I HEAD OUT OF THE OFFICE, not wanting to spend another second with Ash. His rudeness is too much, and I wonder briefly if it had anything to do with Ember kissing me.

I need to leave. As I head down the hallway, convinced that I'm going to get Ember to take me home, I come across photos perched on a cupboard along the wall.

I stop in front of one photo and notice the two boys with a woman who must be their mother. Her long blond hair is flicked behind her shoulders, and the two boys are cuddled against her cheeks. Three grinning faces. Were they out having a picnic? Or was it a celebration, perhaps a birthday?

I notice her eye color upon closer inspection. It's strange—one blue and one green—and I wonder if that's why the boys have different eye colors.

One person is missing in the photo—their father. Come to think of it, he's in none of the pictures. My brows furrow in confusion as I make my way through each picture, and I note there isn't a man in any of them. Perhaps he's the one behind the camera.

Growing up, you think your parents are invincible. It's as if they're superheroes and you think they'll always be there. You expect them to be. At least, I suppose until you're married with kids of your own. But death doesn't have a timeframe. It comes when you least expect it. And when it visits, it leaves breath-stealing pain in its wake.

What would it be like if I was never able to see my father again? Not even in a photo—a captured memory. What if they'd all burned down along with the rest of the store?

My heart suddenly hurts for both boys that they don't have something to hold onto, a tangible thing reminding them of their dad, I can't imagine how much it must hurt. I feel guilty for being so angry at Ash. His pain isn't something he hides on the inside like his brother. Ash exerts his rage outwardly, and I wonder if he's like that with everyone. If so, that's a dangerous thing to do. Because you could be pushing someone away who may inadvertently help you.

When I arrive in the living room, I find Ember sitting

on the sofa, his left ankle resting on his right knee. His green eyes meet mine and the corner of his mouth quirks when he sees me.

"He told you to leave him alone," he says before taking a sip from the glass he's holding. It's not a question. He knows his brother so well.

I nod.

"That's one thing about Ashton; he prefers being on his own."

"Unless he has a woman in a hotel room?" The snarky comment tumbles from my lips without me thinking. I shouldn't be jealous. I was one of those women, but for reasons I don't want to explain, I do feel envious that he'd rather spend time with a stranger and pay them than to be here with us.

He laughs. "My brother enjoys being around anyone who doesn't allow him to feel. Emotion and Ash don't go hand in hand, and that's how he's always been."

I don't know why his explanation troubles me. I feel as if I want to force Ash to feel something, anything. He may be a stranger to me, but this *want* I feel for him is all so new, so strange to me.

"Why?" I close the distance between us, aware that I'm delving into their lives. Even though I've seen their family photos, seeing them when they were young, there is so much more to learn about them both. This house holds secrets, too; I can feel it.

"Ash has gone through something I'll never understand. He took my father's death harder than I did," Ember tells me, lifting a tumbler which he swirls around before meeting my gaze. "Not to say, I didn't love my father, but he was a difficult man."

"And you were closer to your mother?"

Ember offers a solemn smile. "She wasn't well when we were younger, and by the time we were about ten, we lost her. My father was never quite the same after that."

"That's understandable. When you love someone and lose them, I mean . . ."

He rises before stalking closer to me, making my heartbeat speed up. He takes my hand in his as he leads me through the house without a word. We make our way down the hallways until we reach the back of the house. We stop outside a dark wooden door, and after Ember pushes it open, he steps aside, allowing me to enter the space.

Intrigue and suspense grip me in their hold, and as much as I should tell him I want to go home, I can't help but want to also be here and figure out what's going on.

Even in the dimly lit room, I can smell the paint and the chemicals used to clean the brushes. Ember flicks the light on, and I'm met with walls of canvasses of color screaming at me from every corner of the room.

Strolling through the studio, I take in each art piece. The brushstrokes are wild, scattered splotches of color along with strokes of hues that can only be described as violent and stormy.

"These are incredible," I murmur, wanting to reach out and touch them. I twine my fingers from my left hand in my right, to stop myself.

"When my father died, I spent my nights in here. I got lost in the smell of paint because it was the only thing that kept me sane." Sadness drips from his every word. His voice is heavy with emotion, and I find myself drawn to him.

But why do I feel like that?

I've lived through the same agony, and no words can make it better. Not even now, when I feel like I have a chance. I'm still lost, and there's nothing that will ever heal the pain in my chest.

"I wish I could tell you the heartache lessens," I say, not meeting his gaze. But instead, I focus on the paintings on the wall. One catches my attention. It's a dark canvas, black and gray, but in the center are three beautiful rosebuds. The tips of their petals are charred, and they've lost their color.

The center flower is larger than the other two. I can't stop my fingertips from brushing over the rose. I feel the electricity shoot through me the moment I come into contact with the paint as if it's alive. "This one . . ."

"I painted that not long after our father passed away," he tells me, and I notice how close he is. The warmth of his body is against my back, and as if the painting is radiating its own heat, and I feel cocooned, nestled in the effortless emotion.

In this house, just like the rose in this painting, I feel like I'm amongst the ashes and embers.

EMBER

SEEING HER IN A ROOM, NOT EVEN ASHTON HAS ever entered is jarring. This was my salvation. If it weren't for my art, I might have turned to drinking and whores like my brother did. But then again, he was always more like our father than I was.

I spent my time making love to the canvas, while Ash lost himself in women. We both had our addictions, so to speak, and I think we've come out okay on the other side. I hope Katerina can as well.

I hate the thought of her selling her body to make ends meet. And I'm praying with all I have she'll sign the agreement tonight. Not only for my selfish reasons or the guilt that eats away at me but because she needs this like she needs her next breath.

Kat is still staring at the painting, and I'm too close. I want to inhale her fragrance and tell her all our secrets.

Even the ones that involve her, but I know the moment she learns why she's really here, and who Ash and I are, we'll lose her. And that thought only solidifies my resolve. She can never know.

"Do you like painting?" I question instead as I turn to the small desk I keep against the wall. The chair that I settle on is rickety, but I love its authenticity of how it fits in here perfectly. It's how I would picture an art studio in the south of France. Hidden on a small wine farm overlooking the fields would be a small room where a painter ends up going mad, inhaling the fumes every day and drinking himself into a stupor every night.

"Art has been a love of mine for a long time," she tells me. Her back is still to me, and I watch her move through the easels and canvasses. "My father bought me my first sketchbook."

Her voice is a whisper, filled with regret, and I find myself leaning forward, urging her with my mind to continue.

She turns and smiles as though she's heard me. "I was addicted, seeing what I had in my mind come to life with a pencil and piece of paper. I'd always wanted to paint, to learn about the greats."

"Well, you will be. Just tell the dean what you'd like to

major in, and he'll make it happen." My assurance gives her pause, and I can't help but smile. She's intoxicating.

"Why have you taken me on as a project?" she questions suddenly. Her head tips to one side and her brows furrow as she regards me with those steel-gray eyes. Her pink lips purse as she watches me for my response.

"Like we explained, our father—"

"But I'm nothing to your father. Or even you and Ash," she interrupts. "I just find it strange. I may agree to the scholarship you're offering, but I don't know if I can live with you. Not because I'm not grateful for what you're doing for me, but I can't allow myself to trust something that doesn't make sense."

I know she's right and I nod. Her eyes are on me, boring through me. I want to smile, to tell her she's safe and that she's here to heal Ashton. And to help me with the choice I have to make that I have already made, but I don't. I ponder my response because nothing I can say will make her trust us. She needs to *see* it. "Are you not used to people wanting to help you?" I arch a brow at her.

She shakes her head, and I set the glass down. Rising from my seat, I round the desk and eat up the distance between us. Our bodies are close and as much as I want to kiss her, to steal all her doubts and replace them with promises, I know I can't be the one to do it.

"We'll show you that you can trust us. If you'd like to go home now you can, but dinner is ready, and we should eat before you leave. Stay?" I plead, cupping her face in my hands. I hold her steady so she can't turn away. "Even if it's only for one meal." I gaze at her, look right through her eyes that remind me of a cloudy sky on a chilly fall day. The promise of rain lingers in her gaze about to extinguish the fire between all three of us.

"Dinner. Then I need to go home."

I nod, stepping away from her.

"And that trust you want me to allow you," she tells me. "Give it time." Her voice is small, filled with wariness and pain. I want to shove my hand into her body, to steal her hurt and never allow it near her again. I want to eliminate every doubt in her mind.

I hear the click of the door, but I don't acknowledge Ashton.

His body is behind hers in a second, and I notice her gasp when his hands land on her hips. She's between us with nowhere to run and nowhere to hide.

"Kitten," he coos in her ear. "I'm sorry for being an asshole."

She glances at him over her shoulder, causing me to

release her face from my hold. "You can't apologize for being yourself."

Her sharp retort causes him to chuckle, and I can't help laughing as well. He's going to have his hands full soon enough, and I'm glad she's not someone who will lie back and let him walk all over her.

"Touché, Kitten." He presses a kiss on her lips, and she allows him to. My plan is falling into place perfectly. My brother is a creature of habit. The moment he saw us in the kitchen, I knew he'd want to lay claim, and I'm sure he's not going to mess this up. He can't.

Having my brother enter my studio sets me at ease. He's never showed an interest in my painting, and I always thought it would gnaw at me, but I find I like it.

"You're joining us for dinner?" I question Ash, who nods in response. He steps back, allowing us all to move from the studio and into the hallway. Shutting the door, I follow Katerina and my brother through the house and into the dining room, which is already decked out with plates and glasses for wine and water.

Ashton pulls out a chair for our guest, who slips into it as if she was made to be here in our home. I watch them for a moment until Ash looks over at me, offering me a sobering nod. He gestures for me to sit beside her, and he finds a seat opposite us. My confusion whirls inside my gut because if there's one thing I know about my brother, it's that he always goes for the girl.

Soon we're served by Greta, our cook, and when she notices Kat, she offers a friendly smile. The ladies chat for a moment, but my gaze is locked on Ash. I should confess and tell him everything. He deserves to know what I found out last week. But I shake my head, clearing my mind of the anxious thoughts when Katerina picks up an olive and plops it between her plump lips. The motion has both of us staring at her as if she's an exotic animal we've never seen before.

When she notices us, her gaze flits between us, and she furrows her brows. "What?" She smiles, looking at me for an answer.

"You shouldn't do that around us, Kitten," Ash says, flicking his napkin and smoothing it onto his lap. "You're far too tempting." He picks up a fork and spears a potato before popping it into his mouth.

Our dinner is comfortable. There's nothing that makes my heart happier than seeing my brother and Kat banter. And every now and then, I entertain her with a story about Ash when he was a boy.

As soon as our meal is over, I offer my good night and

head up to my room. Ash will take Katerina home, and I need to do something my brother can't see. The pain is shooting through me again, and I'm dizzy when I reach my bedroom.

Shutting the door, I lean against the wood and close my eyes. I can't hide it for much longer. He'll notice it. Ashton is observant, and I know soon, the truth will spill free.

KATERINA

WE DROVE BACK TO MY HOUSE IN SILENCE, AND I didn't push Ash for any more information. Even though he sat beside me in the town car, he didn't make a move to touch me.

It's dark, and I should put the light on, but I don't. The bedroom is silent when Ash and I enter. My small room is nothing like the one they would offer me, but I know I can't accept that right now.

"Have you thought about the offer yet?" Ash asks after shutting my bedroom door.

I turn to regard him and nod. "I have. The scholarship I'll agree to, but I can't live with you and Ember. Not yet." Something isn't sitting right. They're both hiding the truth from me, and I'm determined to discover it.

He's silent for a moment, and I wonder if he's about to retract his offer. Honestly, I pray he doesn't. But even if he does, I know I'll be able to work and save my money until I'm ready.

"Accepted. We can sign right now," he tells me, pointing to the folder containing the contract.

I realize what a long day it's been and can't stop the yawn that falls free from my lips. "I'm sorry."

"You've had a lot to think about. Let's get that signed, and I'll leave you to get some rest." Ash smiles, gesturing again to the document in front of me.

"Are you going to the bar after this?" I don't know why I question him.

"Curiosity killed the cat," he utters, but he doesn't come near me. His blue eyes turn dark.

"The cat has nine lives," I retort, trying to play off what I was actually asking—is he going to be with another woman tonight.

"Katerina," he says my name with a shake of his head. When Ash stalks closer, the air suddenly feels too heavy to pull into my lungs. He's so handsome in his crisp white button-up and black slacks. I can't help drinking him in like a fine wine. "I don't like being questioned about my life, but . . ."

"I wasn't—"

"You're so beautiful, so sweet, I'd hate to deny you

everything in that document and let you continue whoring your beautiful body out to strangers."

His words sting, burning like poison as they travel through me.

"Anything you need I can make happen, but let me make one thing clear," he says, reaching me. His body is molded to mine, the heat of his skin burns through the material of his T-shirt, turning me molten, igniting need that tightens low in my stomach. "If I ever catch you kissing anyone but me again, I'll lose my shit, and you'll both pay dearly."

"Why?" I bite out. "What do I mean to you? I walked into your office, and you threw me out." I don't know where the confidence comes from, but it seems to jar us both.

He doesn't move. His gaze is locked on mine. I notice the flicker of something in his eyes, and his brows furrow in confusion when he asks, "Do you think I don't want you?"

"Ash, I've spent years reading people. I know when I'm not wanted. And you've made it very fucking clear I'm nothing more than a charity case."

"Do not fucking call yourself that, Kitten." He steps closer to me, causing my nipples to peak instinctively against my thin tank top. They brush against his warm, hard chest, and I can't stop this need I have for him.

A desperate desire swirls low in my gut, and my concentration falters for a moment before I step back, but realize my mistake immediately when I feel the desk at my ass.

The corner of his mouth tilts, and he leans into me, caging me against the smooth wooden surface. His lips are so close and as much as I want to move away, I can't.

No. That's not true. I don't want to.

Because as much as I want to deny it, I crave Ash.

But what if he's lying?

Can you ever have your cake and eat it too?

"Ash."

"Kitten," he coos, his voice low and drenched with desire that I feel from the tips of my toes to the top of my head.

I should push him away, but the moment my palms land on his skin, I know I've made a mistake. Electricity sizzles through me, zapping every nerve in my body. "Please."

"Please kiss you? Please touch you? Or please fuck you? Because those are the only choices, I'm offering." He's not joking, his hard gaze on me, striking a match which only seems to burn deeper within my very soul.

I want to say all three. I feel drunk when his lips whisper along my cheek. It's a heady feeling as if I finished a bottle of wine and have no control over my body or my actions. As if Ashton is the puppet master, and I'm merely the toy on a string.

"I . . . I . . . can't . . ."

"You can." He smirks, the corner of his mouth kicking up, and I'm met with his dimples as lust dances like a blue flame in his eyes. The emotion swims within the depths of his orbs, and I feel myself drowning every second I'm lost in them.

"Ash, don't do this," I plead, but even to my own ears, there's no conviction in my words. I want to push him away, but I want to drag him closer. *What's wrong with me?*

He presses his lips against my thrumming heartbeat, which turns my body molten with want and need. The softness of his lips, the heat of his breath fan over me, and the way he presses me against the desk makes every inch of me burn up.

"Tell me, Kitten." He urges, the ridge of his bulge taunting me, causing me to whimper. "Tell me how you want me to stop." The rasp in his voice is warm, trickling over me like syrup, and I can't stop licking my lips, needing to taste every drop.

"Ash . . ."

"Fuck this, Kat. You can't deny you want me," he tells me the one thing I've wanted to admit—I do want him. He doesn't wait for me to refuse him anymore. His lips land on mine. They mold to me as if he was made to fit against me, and perhaps even inside me. He pushes me backward, and my ass settles on the wooden desktop.

The hard bulge of his cock presses against my core, making me whimper into his mouth. I want so much to feel him, to take my shorts off and beg him to make my memories go away, to make the pain go away, but I don't.

His hands trail up my thighs before gripping onto my hips and holding me against him. I can't move, and I don't want to. I'm torn, ripped in two, and there's nothing I can do to stop it.

His tongue sweeps into my mouth lazily as if he's merely tasting, testing the waters, but the moment my hands twine around his neck and I tug him closer, he must realize that there's no way I can deny him.

I want Ash Addington with a fire so fierce, it threatens to burn me to nothing.

The heat of him mingled with the warmth of me turns the air in the room stifling. Desire consumes us.

When Ash finally pulls away, my lips tingle and my body trembles, but he doesn't step back. He doesn't move.

"You're far too intoxicating," he informs me with a wry smirk on his full dusky lips, and I revel in his beauty. "I can't deny you." His confession is a raspy whisper. Each word grips my heart.

"And I can't deny you as much as I want to," I tell him honestly. He's someone who can give me a life I never thought would ever be possible, but it's more than that.

"I want to kiss you all the fucking time. I want to taste you, and I want to hear you scream my name the moment you come on my cock." He voices his desires, filthy words which make me squirm on the top of my desk.

"You're still an asshole who pushes people away," I tell him.

"I never once denied it, Kitten." He chuckles, his hands still caging me in. I'm caught by the man, but I'm not a prisoner; I'm here because I want to be.

"No, you didn't. But . . . This is . . . Ember is . . ."

"My brother likes you a lot. And if you want him, then tell me now. But just know this," he utters in a low gravelly tone, finally stepping back and allowing me to breathe. "I don't give up. I want you. I wanted you the moment I first laid my eyes on you, and even though I knew he'd be a better match, I played my hand."

"It's you, Ash. I want you." It's true and real, and my heart is thudding so hard I'm scared it's going to tear through my chest. I want to feel wanted, but I need it to be real. Not because he's paid me, not because he's bought me for the night. And right now, Ash is showing me every emotion I'm feeling—confusion, desire, affection, and yearning.

Ash smiles, his face illuminated by the dim light of the bulb hanging overhead. "Then it's me you'll have."

I get lost in his promise for a moment. It's everything I want.

"I've never . . . I've not done the dating and girlfriend thing before." He grins. "But I guess I could try."

"My focus is my future, Ash. As much as I want you, I also need the money," I tell him. "But I won't be here as someone you've paid to be in your life."

"Life doesn't afford us many choices, Kitten," Ash finally says. I'm not sure what he means. I'm about to ask when he continues. "But you have one, and you've taken it. You're not here for Ember or me; you're here for your future." I get a glimpse of his true heart. There's no denying he's felt pain, but at least he's honest.

Pain will fray you. It will rip you to shreds.

And love is the only thing that can put you back together.

I know Ember's love for his brother healed him somewhat. But Ash is still torn, and I wonder if I could ever mend him.

"And you're willing to try? For real?" I watch him for a moment, wanting him to tell me I'm his. I'm so scared, so fucking afraid of what's coming, but if there's one thing my parents taught me, it's to take a chance but keep your eyes wide open.

"I told you, Kitten. I want you." He smiles. "You're strong, you're independent, but every now and then, you have to admit you need help. Our agreement has nothing to do with us."

I seek his gaze for a lie, for the punchline to some joke that he's playing on me, but I find none. I'm staring up at him; he's still so close. His spicy cologne holds me, hostage, swirling around me, and I know I'll never get that intoxicating smell out of my head.

"Okay," I finally utter.

"Tomorrow is Friday, let's spend the afternoon together and get to know each other better. Perhaps we can go for dinner." His smile is everything. I find myself nodding.

"I'd like that."

A date with Ash. Who would've thought?

KATERINA

"WHY CAN'T I LOOK?" I QUESTION WITH A giggle. Ash collected me at home and blindfolded me. Normally I'd be nervous, but he's given me no reason to be scared. He even told Isobel where we're going, though he swore her to secrecy. She smiled, offered me a wink, and told me to misbehave.

I don't know how long we've been driving but I can feel the heat of the sun on my legs, so I know it is still afternoon. I opted for a pair of denim cutoffs and a tank top since it's rather warm today.

The moment the car stops, I want to tug off the material covering my eyes, but Ash growls beside me. "If you dare pull that off, I'll spank you," he utters in my ear, causing a shiver to rattle through me. The car door slams and moments later, mine is opened and Ash's hands helping me from my seat.

He walks me through what I'm guessing is a parking lot, and then we're told to go through. I have no idea what we're *going through*, but my heartbeat is erratic when we come to a stop and Ash tugs the blindfold from around my head.

I'm met with lush greenery, and the view is utterly breathtaking. I don't know where we are, but I'm speechless.

"Welcome to the Japanese Tea Garden," Ash whispers in my ear. The heat of his breath warms me inside out, and I'm tempted to turn and kiss him on those full lips.

"Ash, this is incredible," I murmur.

He laces his fingers through mine, and he leads me through the garden at a languid pace. We stop and look at every tree, every beautiful flower, and when pausing at a large fern which sweeps overhead shading us, I glance over at him. "I thought you didn't date?"

"I don't. I never saw the need," he tells me earnestly and my stomach bottoms out. *Why do I feel so sad that he's just said that?* I shouldn't feel like this for him. *Should I?* He doesn't look at me, but he continues, "All my life I've been happy with my brother being my confidante. Having a girl hampering for my attention is something I couldn't justify."

"And now?" The question falls from my lips without my thinking about it, but I can't stop it now. I watch and wait for him to respond.

"My feelings aren't set in stone, Kat. I can't tell you if I'll ever change who I am, but this"—he takes my hand and presses a kiss to it— "this is something I want to try."

My heart pitter-patters at his confession, and I can't stop the stupid smile that curls my lips. "So, you'll take me on more dates then?"

My question makes him smile. His perfect dimples appear the moment I ask it. And I know I'm pushing my luck. Ash may be giving parts of himself to me, but I need to be careful. He could shut down at any time. And that makes me wary.

"Perhaps."

"You're rather indecisive, take a moment to step outside your comfort zone once in a while," I tease, giggling and squealing when he pulls me into his arms and tickles my stomach. The other people visiting the garden either offer smiles or frowns at our display, but I don't care. I feel happy.

"Don't tease me, Kitten," Ash growls in my ear once more, causing my cheeks to burn and my body to heat at the timber of his voice. I don't know why, but when he speaks in that gravelly tone, I want him to touch me, undress me, and make love to me.

He straightens, helping me up, and then we start walking side by side again. "What about the other girls you've fucked?" I whisper. "Did none of them make you want to take them on a date? Or am I special?"

Ash's blue gaze lands on mine. It's as if he's searching for something in my eyes, but whatever he's looking for, he doesn't find. At least, I don't think he does.

He turns to me, fully facing me. He cups my cheeks in his hands, holding me steady and stealing my breath without doing anything at all.

"You're inquisitive, Kitten." He smiles before leaning in close and brushing his lips across mine. His heat sears me. It warms me. Cocoons me in a protectiveness that wraps itself around me, and I can't explain it.

When he pulls away, I say, "I just want to know you."

"Why?"

Tipping my head to the side, I reach for his face and run my thumb over his cheek. The stubble scratches at the pad of my finger, and I smile. "Because . . . I don't know." My answer may not be something he wants to hear. *Should I tell him? If I do, will I scare him off?* I don't want that. No. I want Ash in my life, and that thought frightens me more than it should.

He's bad and good all wrapped up in a perfect package, and I wonder if it unravels, what I'll find inside.

"You do know, and I'll make you tell me soon enough," he counters, causing a ripple of fear and need to trail through me. "Let's get ice cream."

His grin is playful, and he tugs me along through the trees and flowers until we happen upon a small café. We order our sugar cones—I get a double chocolate scoop, and Ash smirks at his large scoop of choc mint, which makes me gag.

"That's so gross." I squeal when he presses the cold dessert onto the tip of my nose. Happiness bubbles in my chest. I haven't felt this light and carefree for a long while. And it's Ash who's offering it to me.

I wonder what the cost will be.

My mind, soul, or heart?

We meander through the park for a while longer before Ash glances at me. "Ready to go home?" He watches me for a moment, and I nod.

"Yeah, I have to meet with Maria and tell her I'll be studying."

He walks me back to the car in comfortable silence. Once we're on our way, I ask, "So, you have meetings tomorrow?"

"Yes, I have a few, but more than that I have a board meeting coming up which I need to prep for. I need to make sure I have briefings from each department before that."

"Sounds tiring," I remark, causing him to chuckle.

"It can be."

It doesn't take us long to get home, and soon I'm sad that our date is at an end. Ash walks me to the door, his body close to mine. He tips my chin up, causing my gaze to lock on his.

He presses a kiss to my lips, and I snake my arms around his neck to pull him closer. It doesn't take long for him to deepen the kiss and I'm whimpering when I feel every hard ridge of him against me. His tongue sweeps along mine, and I suck it, eliciting a groan from him which makes me smile.

He steps back, and I'm cold. His heat no longer covers me. "Dinner on Saturday at the gala. I'll send a dress for you tomorrow. Sign the agreement. And then get some rest."

He follows me deeper into the house and to my bedroom. Once there, I turn to the desk, signing my life away. I read through the agreement a few times last night, and I'm sure this is the right thing now. At least he's agreed to let me stay here, instead of moving in with them. Perhaps one day. Just not now.

I'm giving my life to a man who's offering me a dream.

I just pray it doesn't turn into a nightmare.

I keep my home, and I get to study. No strings.

Ash signs as well, and it's done. He offers me a kiss on the cheek, and my skin heats from where his lips touched. "Good night, Kitten. I'll see you on Saturday."

"Okay. I'll be ready."

ASH

HOW CAN TWENTY-FOUR HOURS FEEL LIKE A lifetime?

After the other night in her room, I've been aching to feel her against me once more. When I told Katerina I'd collect her, and she could change at the mansion, she agreed. The moment she walks down the stairs, my body is rigid with shock.

I've seen Katerina naked. I've seen her dressed in beautiful dresses on the nights I'd paid for her company, but this . . . Nothing has prepared me for the moment she reaches me in her silver floor-length silk dress.

Her slight curves are encased in the soft material. Her breasts look incredible with the scooped neck, and the thin straps that hang over her shoulders offer an erotic, yet sensual view of just enough skin to have my cock responding with a throb.

"So?" she questions as she spins around.

I regard her with hunger. The lace offers glimpses of her skin, but it's not crude. She is elegantly sexy. I'm tempted to rip the damn thing off and take her against the wall.

Clearing my throat, I offer, "You look . . . incredible." This raw honesty is something I've never given another woman before. All the arm candy I've ever had draped over me were whores. Women I didn't care for, only there to get my dick wet. But with Katerina, I'm so fucked because as much as I know, I want to keep her for myself, I can't.

"I'm nervous," she confesses when she meets my gaze. Her body is trembling with anxiety, and I can't stop myself from pulling her into my arms. She's small, shorter than me, and slim. I engulf her in my hold, and when I look up, I notice Ember at the top of the stairs in his tuxedo.

"We'll be with you the whole time," I tell her. Stepping back, I tip her head up with my finger under her chin and meet her gaze. "Either Ember or I will be right beside you. You have nothing to be scared of."

"I know, I just . . . I want this so much." I realize she's talking about school and getting to study, but it almost feels as if she's talking about us—me and my brother. I'm

218

still in awe knowing this woman wants me. As much as I should let her go, to be with Ember instead, I find myself tumbling freely into her orbit every day.

"You look lovely, sweetheart," Ember tells her when he reaches us. He places his fingers on the small of her back, and I turn to walk out of the house. The car is waiting, and I wonder just how this evening is going to play out.

A few nights ago, she confessed she wanted me, and I'm ready. I truly am.

All I need to do now is tell her the truth.

Once we're all seated in the town car, it pulls out before taking the road toward the university. Deafening silence surrounds us. Kat's gaze is on the lights flitting by, and I hope she's thinking about our conversation, more importantly, our kiss.

It was a beautiful moment, feeling her lips on mine. For the first time, I recognized desire coursing through me. It was different. I didn't want to forget anything; I wanted to be present.

I jerked off thinking about her this morning. And again just before I got dressed for dinner. I came hard in the shower, imagining her heat against me and my mouth tasting every inch of her.

I glance at Ember, who seems comfortable with

Katerina and me sitting beside each other. I know he's hiding something. I just wish I knew what.

The car pulls into the lot alongside other expensive vehicles. When we come to a stop, I'm out of the car and offering my hand to Kat before Ember can move. I don't know why I'm doing this shit, but I find myself needing to prove to them both that I'm not an asshole. Even if it's only for tonight.

Kat's arm is looped through my left. Ember steps up beside her, and she takes his right arm. I know there'll be questions, perhaps even comments about why she's with us, but right now, all I want everyone to know is... she's ours.

I feel eyes on us as we move through the crowds. When we reach the doorway, we're greeted with friendly nods from the staff.

The moment we step into the hall where the dinner is being held, I hear a soft gasp from Kat. "This is amazing. I didn't know it would be this exquisite," she says, and I can hear the smile on her face even though I'm not looking at her. I must agree with her. I've never seen a gala dinner at a university this incredibly decked out before.

It's magical.

Gold lights are shimmering from every inch of the

ceiling. The tiled floor looks like it's alight with bulbs underneath, even though I know it's not. There's a band sitting at the far end of the room. Tables are positioned around a large dance floor which as I recall from the last few I've attended will be filled with bodies swaying late into the night.

Everyone in the room is dressed in tuxedos and evening dresses. The women look like they're ready for a runway show, and the men appear to have walked off the pages of a goddamn magazine.

We're ushered to a table where I notice the Dean, Reginald Harrington, seated beside his wife.

"Ah, Ashton, Ember welcome. Your father was a great man, and one of my closest friends. Having you both in attendance really is an honor." He smiles, rising from his seat to shake our hands, grinning. The air is filled with excitement and anticipation, but when his eyes land on Katerina, there's a slight falter in his expression which I pray she doesn't notice. "It's so lovely to see you, Katerina."

"And you too, Dean Harrington."

"I hope you'll enjoy the presentation we have this evening. Addington and Associates have always been a great supporter of the scholarship fund," he informs her, pressing a kiss to her cheek.

Once everyone has been introduced, we settle in, Kat between myself and Ember, and I focus my gaze on the dean who's watching Kat with curiosity. He knows. There's no doubt in my mind that he recollected what happened, and now he knows why I've asked for her to be admitted to the university. And I'm confident the understanding between us will be kept quiet as to why I'm paying.

"So, Katerina," he says. "Are you excited to be starting school here?" His focus is unwaveringly on the beauty between my brother and I.

KATERINA

SOMETHING CLICKS INSIDE ME. I KNOW THIS MAN knows more about me than he should. I'm not sure what it is, perhaps gut instinct, and I feel pressure to respond with the right answer.

My mouth opens, and just before I reply, Ash settles his hand on my thigh, offering me a reassuring squeeze.

"I'm looking to major in art and music," I tell the dean with a smile. "Two of my passions. They are both the subject my parents introduced me to at a young age, and I'd like to honor them by getting my diploma in both subjects."

"Well, we offer a wonderful creative program, and someone who enjoys the arts is most certainly welcome here. And if you don't mind me asking . . . Your parents?"

"I . . . They passed away a while ago," I tell him, swallowing back my emotion. *Don't cry. Easier said than done.* "I lost them when I was sixteen." I finally say. It may be silly, but it's as though confessing something so excruciating, only cracks me further.

"I'm so sorry to hear that, darling," the woman beside the dean utters, her hand on her chest in shock, but the dean doesn't seem surprised by my admission.

"That's terrible," he tells me, but I know he's lying. Confusion settles in my gut, and I wonder for a moment if Ash told him about my past. But that shouldn't be something that comes up unless it hinders my schooling, which it hasn't.

"I think we need to talk about the future of the courses at the university," Ashton utters, his voice dripping with malice, perhaps he's angry at the dean delving into my past. "Because the donations are coming in, but dean, didn't you mention you'd be needing help with the expansion of the music department?"

Something flickers between the two men, causing the air to linger with a heaviness that seems to stifle everything from the music to the chatter. But it's only my perception. The moment I look away from their interaction, everyone seems oblivious to what's going on at our table.

"Dean Harrington." A young girl rushes up to the table with a bright smile. Her gaze lands on Ash and then

Ember, and I recognize her reaction to them. It's the same one I have each time I walk into their space. "We need you on stage for the welcome," she tells the dean with a smile.

"I'll be there in a moment." Rising from his seat, he nods toward us before he makes his way up to the stage and we're left with his wife at the table. Ash's hand is still on my thigh, holding onto me like I'm about to disappear.

"Good evening, ladies and gentlemen, and a special welcome to our new students." The dean smiles from the stage. The band sits silently behind him, presumably waiting for their moment to shine. "This evening, we have our scholarship students from the Addington fund who are going to be joining us this semester. Each student is special, chosen for a reason. I normally call each of our youngsters up on stage, but this year I'd like to do something different."

"What is he doing?" Ash questions the woman who's seated beside him.

The wife of the dean smiles as if she's proud of her husband. "He's giving the intros for the students who are joining us, explaining to our sponsors why they were chosen."

Both Ash and Ember still beside me; they're rigid. A slideshow pops up on the screen with the face of a man

I recognize instantly. He's exactly like I remember him in a three-piece suit and white shirt, with a smile that could melt butter.

My heart leaps into my throat as the speech continues. "Mr. Addington has always believed in giving back to our community, and when he came up with the idea of offering a handful of students the opportunity to study further, we were thankful for his contribution. Each year we have a random selection process, but we have a student especially chosen by Ashton and Ember Addington. Welcome to the lovely Katerina Nielsen, who will be the star pupil from the Addington Fund."

He points in the direction of our table and as both men beside me rise, all eyes land on me, causing my body to shudder as I push my chair backward. It squeaks along the floor, but I ignore the sound, rushing from the room with Ashton behind me. He calls to me as I make my way through the empty hallways. When I reach the ladies restroom, I push the door open and shove my way inside.

Thankfully, it's empty, and I bend over the sink, my arms shaking as I hold myself up by my hands on the metal counter. Inhaling deep breaths, I try to focus, but I feel the bile rising in my throat, and I expel my lunch into the sink.

When the door flies open, I don't need to turn

around. I know Ash is here, his spicy cologne envelops me. He's at my back, reaching for me before I shrug him off. I don't know why he chose me specifically, but knowing his father was the man who tried to help me has me scared and nervous.

"Kitten," Ash starts, but I swing my arm out, pushing him away from me.

"Don't fucking *kitten* me." My voice is venom. "You knew who I was. Didn't you?" I meet those cerulean eyes, finding the lies dancing in them. For the first time since I met Ash, I see dishonesty in his face.

"Listen to me—"

"No, I will not listen to your lies. Not this time. You may have fooled me before, and yes, I may have been stupid enough to believe you, but this time is different. I'm not taking your charity," I tell him, shoving my way out of the restroom. I slam into Ember who's waiting outside. "What? You're here to try to calm me down as well?"

"Just listen to us, please, Katerina," Ember says calmly as if I'm a wayward child who needs to be put in the naughty corner. Any other time I may have agreed, but they lied. The acted as if they didn't know me. They made me believe my secrets were mine to keep, but that was all a big fat lie.

Ignoring both brothers, I head down the hallway and out the main door. My heels click on the steps as I race toward the parking lot. There aren't many cabs close by, and I wonder just how far I'll have to walk to find one. I can go back to Isobel. She'll be able to help me.

I'm suddenly lifted off my feet and spun over a suited shoulder. "Put me the fuck down," I bite out, but Ash ignores me as he saunters through the lot. When we reach our car, I can't help gasping as he slides me down his body before I'm shoved onto the leather seat.

He settles in beside me, with Ember already sitting opposite us. Both brothers watch me try to open the door, but they must've put the child lock on because I can't do it.

"Let me out," I grit through clenched teeth, pinning Ash with a glare, which only earns me a chuckle. The asshole is actually laughing at me. "Ash, let me the fuck out."

"And where exactly would you go in the dead of night on your own when you're nowhere near the city?" he questions me, amusement lacing his tone which only further infuriates me.

"That was uncalled for." I change tactic. "My family has nothing to do with who I am and why I'm here. I could've been anyone."

"You didn't want people to know you're just a beautiful girl who lost her parents, but you were happy to work the streets? Is that what you wanted? To be a whore for hire while you studied?" Ash's words are pure poison. Disdain drips from every utterance, stilling me for a moment.

Even though I'm still angry, he has a point. And fuck if that doesn't annoy me.

"I'm . . . I just didn't want the whole goddamn university knowing I'm a charity case for you and your brother. I need to spend the next four years there. And why didn't you tell me who your father really was?"

The corner of Ash's mouth purses, his gaze darkens with fury, before he responds, "I don't think you want to know."

EMBER

HE WANTS TO LIE.
I know my brother; he's exactly like our father. I wish she'd look at me, just at this moment. I pray she turns to me and asks, but even if she did, I don't know if I would be able to tell her. I want so much for her to learn the truth. With a quick glance at Ash, I can tell he realizes he has a decision to make.

"What do you mean?" he asks, opting for the most straightforward response in this situation.

She looks at me, her gaze imploring me to respond, begging with merely a glance, and my heart lurches in my chest. It's thudding wildly, needing to leap into her hands and ask for forgiveness. "We didn't want you to run. At least, we just wanted to give you something that he couldn't," I tell her the truth, but still wonder if I sound as guilty as I feel. She doesn't know how much our father tried to make things right. But there was nothing he could've done, nothing would've changed her life.

"What I don't understand is why me? Even though he was in court every day, I don't get what the hell his fascination was with me." She looks like the little girl from two years ago. She reminds me of the child who sat crying on the sofa the night she learned her parents were dead. All I want to do is pull her into my arms and hold her.

"Katerina, listen—"

"No, I'm done listening to your lies. If you're not willing to tell me the truth, then it's best you take me back home now, and you can keep your goddamn agreement." She's adamant.

"Why don't you come to the house with us?"

I know Ash is stalling her. Once we're at the mansion, he'll sit her down and explain that she's not going anywhere. The problem is, I don't know what he's going to tell her about that night.

"Just relax, please, Kitten?" he coos in her ear, hope flaring like wildfire in his eyes as he watches her. I've never seen my brother so enamored with anyone. And it's not the first time I've noticed it since she's come into our lives. "You're welcome to leave when you please. Just give us time to explain."

"I want nothing but the truth." She sits back in resignation, and the rage I noticed earlier in her expression has softened, but only slightly. Tonight, the truth will come out, and I'm not sure I can say goodbye to her.

We sit in silence as the car weaves through the city.

Ash's gaze lingers on mine. I offer him a shake of my head, to leave her be. As the car weaves through the roads, I can't help but stare at her. I feel like I'm taking in my last few glimpses of her, committing her to memory because soon, she'll be gone.

Anger looks good on her.

The fire that runs in her veins turns her body rigid.

When we pull into the driveway, Ash is out of the car, offering his hand to Kat who again only stares him down. But the shrug and chuckle he responds with makes me smile.

He turns away, and I lean forward. "He is trying to help you to shield you from more pain."

"I don't need handouts. He lied to me, which only makes the sting worse. And you—"

"Would you do me the honor of joining me for a drink? I'll explain my side of the story. And then I hope you'll allow Ash to explain his," I urge her, hoping she agrees. If I can give her a taste of why we want her, just a hint of truth, I pray she'll allow us to gift her with the life she deserves.

She offers a nod. It's slight, but it's progress.

I exit the vehicle and wink at my brother who's already heading for the door. I'm the peacemaker, and that worries me. If I'm no longer here one day, who will ensure he doesn't fuck up something else? I love him, but Ash doesn't realize he needs to soften his cold exterior and let her in.

"Your brother is insufferable," Kat utters when she reaches for my hand, and I help her from the car. "I just want the truth, Ember."

"I know, sweetheart," I murmur gently in her ear, hoping to ease her anger and tamper it down somewhat. I lead her into the house, making sure she's right behind me as we head in the opposite direction to where Ash ventured. I need her to listen to me, so she doesn't go running off.

At first, I thought it would be best if she didn't know what happened. But now she's seen our father's face on the screen, it's time some home truths were addressed.

I wait for her to settle on the couch. The way her dress swishes around her thighs makes me smile. A sweet, innocent girl, yet she burns with a fire that seems to tear down both Ash and me.

"Our father wanted to help you." I dive right into my explanation. There's certainly no easy way to tell her; there's nothing that will soothe the ache. "Two days after you were taken into a home, he . . ." My chest tightens when I recall the moment I realized our father was no longer breathing. "Sitting in his favorite office chair, he'd swallowed over twenty different pills that dissolved too quickly to be pumped from his stomach."

"Oh, god, I'm so sorry." Katerina rises, and after taking tentative steps toward me, she places her palms flat on my chest. The heat searing through the material of my shirt is evidence that this girl could have magical powers.

"It happens. Life becomes too much, and at times, we can't face the path we're on. My father was . . . difficult."

"Why am I the object of the Addington obsession? It feels like there's more to the story than just your father being a troubled man." Tears trickle down her cheeks as she regards me. "I just want the lies and secrets to stop."

This is the moment for a confession. I can so easily pull her into my arms and give her the truth she seeks, the one she's clearly craving. But the moment those stormy eyes look up at me, shimmering with unshed tears, I lose all my confidence.

"Sometimes secrets are the only thing holding us together and keeping us from falling apart," I tell her. I reach for her cheek and swipe my thumb along the smooth flesh, feeling the wetness of her emotion.

"But it can also be those secrets that tear your life apart. They could so easily be the same lies you think will keep you safe. But in the end, they're the ones that will destroy you." Her voice is husky, and I watch her slender neck and how it bops when she swallows.

Perhaps she's hiding more than we are.

"I want to know," she tells me.

Nodding, I step back, allowing her to move from the couch and walk toward the door. "Ash has the letters. He's waiting in the office." I offer her a smile, knowing what's about to happen. "I'll see you tomorrow." Perhaps just this small gesture of wanting to give her the truth will keep her here.

I hope it will.

"Thank you." She leaves me to wonder just how much time we'll have with her before she moves on. Once I'm alone in the living room, I wait to hear the click echo from the office door. The moment it sounds, I pour a drink and swallow it down.

At least my father did one thing right, he brought her

to us. Perhaps he knew we'd need her one day, and that she'd need us.

KATERINA

I FIND ASH SITTING ON THE DESK. AFTER SHUTTING the office door, I close the distance between us. He glances up from his drink, and I'm caught breathless. His expression is painted with pain, and his demeanor is rigid, while his gaze burns with guilt. My heart thuds against my chest, attacking my ribs with a vengeance so fierce, it steals my breath.

I'm not sure whether what he's about to tell me will be good. No, scratch that; I know this will be something very, very bad.

He doesn't move for a moment. His fingers gripping the glass so tight, they turn white. He brings the tumbler to his lips and swallows the liquid with a wince. Finally, he looks at me again and gestures for me to sit.

Once I do, he starts.

"The night I learned what my father had done, I had

never felt more ashamed to be an Addington." His voice is heavy with guilt. "Ember was in his studio, and I was out at the hotel," he says, but doesn't elaborate. Thankfully. "When Ember heard the front door, he thought it was me and made his way down the hall. But instead, he saw my father walk into the house," Ash speaks, but I have a feeling this might be the first time he's voicing whatever's been eating away at him.

"Had something happened?" I find myself questioning.

"Ember had been curious; he thought something was very wrong when he went to our dad and tried to offer him help. He said the stench on my father's clothes was so thick, it cloyed at his lungs."

My heart is in my throat. My stomach is doing somersaults, causing me to feel nauseous. I can't swallow. The drumming in my ears is like a foghorn, but even so, I hear every word loud and clear.

"My brother watched him disappear into the office, and he didn't come out. Ember went out to the garage, thinking my father had been in an accident or something. He found the car had ash all over the floorboards."

"What?" A ghost of cold air trickles over me, causing goose bumps to dot my skin, and my spine feels as if ice is surrounding it with each word he utters.

"Dad showered, dressed up in a suit, and headed out which only confused us further. We followed him, and he didn't even know we were there. He'd been beside himself with guilt, or shame, or something that we just didn't know because he wouldn't talk to us. We made it all the way to your house."

My heart begins to crack in that moment—with each fissure, I find it difficult to breathe. I hear it happen as if listening to glass shatter.

"Ember and I watched as you were told your parents were dead." His voice is far away. There's a whooshing sound as the air leaves my lungs in one fell swoop and I'm shaking. My whole body is wrought with fear.

"And . . . and your dad?" I choke out as tears trickle down my cheeks. The pain of living through that again holds me in an icy grip.

Ash looks at me. He watches me for such a long time. I wish I could read his mind to figure out what's going on in there. His cerulean eyes are like glass—wet and shimmering.

I look right into his soul.

Every dark crevice, each light shard, I see it all. I see him.

I finally see Ashton Addington.

"You were there," I murmur. The realization feels like a bucket of ice water has been dumped on me.

"I was," he affirms. "And even then, when I watched you cry, I thought you were the most beautiful girl I'd ever seen." He takes a deep breath before continuing. "When my father died, he'd left me a letter in his home office. He knew I'd find it because I was always the one sitting in there telling him how one day it would all be mine."

"What did the letter say?"

He pulls a crumpled envelope from the pocket of his suit pants. The yellowish paper has creases and small tears as if it's been opened and reopened thousands of times.

"And this was the only letter he left? Did Ember get one as well?"

Ash shakes his head, then pulls out a small white envelope with my name scrawled over the front. It's handwriting I would recognize anywhere. The messy letters in black ink match that of the man who tried to help me.

"Katerina." He takes both my hands. "We think our father was at the store the night your parents died."

"What?" My throat closes, and the hurt from his words unravels my agonizing memories of that night. The images are so clear in my mind, I'm sure it's happening right now. When the one officer placed the glass of water on the table; when I thought of how my mother would've admonished him.

The anger.

The fire that had burned inside me that day.

I recall it with clarity.

"Your father was there. He walked in and told me he would help," I utter. "But he didn't tell me why." I never understood why a stranger had been willing to do so much for a girl he didn't know.

"I think it's time for you to read what happened the night your parents died," Ash tells me gently. I see the truth in his eyes. He knew who I was, all this time. He knew I was that girl.

"Did you plan this? Plan to be my savior?"

"No." He shakes his head adamantly. But I'm already on my feet, clutching both the envelopes before making my way to the staircase. "Please, Kat, just listen to me. I didn't plan . . . I didn't mean . . ."

"You lied to me. You kept this from me since I met you and you have had many chances to tell me who you are."

He shakes his head, his hand shoved into the pocket of his pants. His eyes are almost glowing with frustration when he responds, "I only realized it was you a few months ago—"

"Months? You know what, Ash? You're nothing like your goddamn father. At least he tried to help me without messing with me. He didn't play games; he truly tried." My words choke me up, and when I blink, the tears finally fall free, and I'm crying. My cold shivers intensify.

Ash comes closer, reaching for me, but I step back. I can't be near him, not right now. I can't be in the same room as him, never mind be held by him. Everything seems to be crashing down around me. My heart feels like it's on the ground, lying at his feet, and all he's going to do is burn whatever pieces of me are left.

"Don't, Ash. Don't come near me. I need . . . I want . . . I just need time," I splutter, my body convulsing as I turn and head for the landing. I want to run out of the house but where would I go with no car, no means of getting into the city at night?

"Listen to me, Katerina!" His voice booms around me, stilling me mid-step, and I turn to face him. "I can't lose you. I needed to be honest because I want you in my life. I've never wanted anything more. Why can't you understand? I have never loved someone before. I don't know how to fucking do this, and I just can't lose you."

His anger-filled, guilt-ridden speech shocks me. His body is visibly vibrating with emotion so fierce it grips me in a vise-like hold. The air is thick in this large room and it feels as though something is pressing down on me, holding me hostage.

"Love? You love me? You're not meant to lie to people you love, Ash," I spit out, but my heart hurts the moment I say it because I realize that no matter what he's not told me, no matter how he's kept secrets from me, I love him too.

I never expected it to happen. I was so focused on making my schooling happen, I didn't realize I'd fallen so far down the rabbit hole. And now that I look at him, through all the hurt and anger, I know my broken heart is his. "Why didn't you just tell me the truth?" I question again.

"How the fuck would you have taken it if I had told you my father killed your parents?" he finally retorts with so much rage that I fall to the ground.

KATERINA

MY HEAD IS REELING WITH QUESTIONS THAT replay silently as I clutch the letters Ash gave me. Closing my eyes, I attempt to focus, to ground myself, but there's nothing that can keep the tears at bay. After a long while, I lift my glance at Ash. He's standing there, his expression pained as his eyes shimmer with tears.

"I need time. Please, just let me be," I plead with him.

He opens his mouth but doesn't say anything. With a swift nod, he makes his way to the door and grips the handle. A glance over his shoulder meets my blurry stare. "I won't be far..." Ash blinks, causing the tears that he'd kept at bay to fall. "If you want me."

I hear the click, and I'm alone with my thoughts and the two letters in my hand. I have to read them. For my own sanity, I need to see the words I'm not sure will offer solace or leave me with more questions.

Ash,

When I'm no longer around, and you find this letter, which I'm sure you will, I need to ask you to do something important for me. I trust you will, and I know deep down, your brother will understand why I'm asking this of both of you.

Since you're the eldest, I'm giving you the responsibility of finding someone for me. Once I'm gone, she'll be alone. I've tried so many times to help her, to give her a life that she's worthy of, but the state won, and she went into foster care.

You will take over Addington and Associates, which will give you access to a slew of people who can keep tabs on her. Once she turns eighteen, I want you to find her, watch over her, and make sure she has the life I've given both you and Ember.

I can't explain why, but I need her to know she's not alone. I've included a letter I'd like you to deliver to her. It will offer her the answers she's been looking for, and I hope, that it brings her some sort of clarity and closure.

Son, I haven't ever told you this, but I'm proud of both you and Ember. You're the reason I kept going, but now you're old enough to look after yourselves. You're both responsible adults, more so than I could ever have been. Your mother would've been proud.

There was never a right or wrong time to do this, but just know I love you, Ashton. Don't ever give up searching for the woman who changes you. She'll be the one who will make you see that your life is worth living.

I found mine. It was your mother. When she died, I thought my life was over. I couldn't see past the pain. Losing someone you love will hurt. It will burn you from the inside out until all that's left is rubble. Don't let it take you down.

Love is out there.

You mother once told me something I thought I would share with you. 'Love will always be among Ash and Ember, even when I'm not there.'

And she was right; you both loved me, even at my worst.

Thank you, son.
Dad

Setting the letter on the bed, I close my eyes and breathe deeply. I can't believe their father remembered me on his deathbed. Even after all he'd done to help, he still left a dying wish for his son to find me. I pick up the smaller envelope and tear it at the edge, then pull out the paper which has been folded into three.

On the white card, I find the same scrawl that was on Ash's letter.

Katerina,

I wish I could've done more. Given you more. I just wasn't in the right state of mind to adopt you at the time, although I wish I was. My sons would've enjoyed having a girl in the house. Someone with as much fire and passion as you have. Watching you fall apart, I knew I could never give you the affection you needed. I wasn't even there for my two boys.

I was in the store the evening your parents died. Your dad told me he was working on a large order that needed to be done by morning. I was drunk, telling your father how much I missed my wife. We spoke at length about how she was probably watching me from heaven. She was a good woman, a wonderful wife, and the perfect mother.

In my inebriated state, I spun around and knocked a gas canister on the floor. The hissing sound hit my ears, and I knew something was wrong. I told your father to get your mom—who was tying the bouquet of flowers I'd bought for my late wife—and that was when I saw him. A man passing the window shoved open the door, and he flicked his burning cigarette at the canister before I could think. I pushed him outward, but I was too late.

It wasn't an accident. And it certainly wasn't your parents' fault. It was mine. It was the man dressed in black that I couldn't locate. I spent months exhausting every possible angle. And I still failed.

The place went up in flames. I tried to get back in, but I couldn't because a balustrade had blocked the entrance. I shattered a window, only to have it stoke the fire. It didn't help. I was too weak from the alcohol. I was a mess, and I couldn't save them.

Your mother screamed for me to look at her, and the moment I did, she screeched one word. Your name. Katerina. I watched her disappear in the smoke, and I stood by and did nothing. By the time I turned to the stranger, I had noticed he'd run. To this day, I can't remember his face. Everything was a blur, and for that, I'm guilty. If I wasn't drunk, I could've helped the police find him.

I ran. I fucking ran like the coward I am.

I'm gulping in air, the words are blurry, and somehow, I can see everything clearly in my mind. The small flower store, and my mother calling my name, trying to tell a stranger that I had nobody else in the world.

I focus on the letter once more, swiping at my face.

I tried to help you out of guilt. Out of the pain I'd caused because I blame myself for that fire that stole your parents. Only, I failed at that as well. All I can do is say I'm sorry.

My sons will find you one day, and they'll give this to you.

I wish you well, Katerina, and I hope that the small token

of apology is some sort of penance for my part in your life. My
company, Addington and Associates, will pay for your schooling.
I've left Ashton, my eldest son, in charge, and he will ensure this
is taken care of.

Don't be afraid. You're a strong girl, probably a woman
now.

Let my sons know I love them,
Mr. Addington

I sit in silence. My chest is tight, and my eyes burn with tears. I stare at the wall, attempting to hold the emotion in. I try to keep from breaking. For years, I was alone. For months, I felt as if nothing would ever be okay again.

And now I'm here, with my dreams just within reach, but the men who are offering it to me held this truth from me.

Pushing off the sofa, I find Ember in the kitchen. I think I'm free of Ash, just for the moment, but he enters the space, and soon, both brothers are looking at me.

"He's innocent," I tell them, glancing at Ember, then Ash. "In his letter to me, he explained what happened. He was buying flowers for your mother's grave." They both visibly relax their tightened jaws. Ash's eyes flicker with emotion. Tears pool in them, and I want to go to him.

"Thank you," Ash murmurs.

"It doesn't change the fact that you lied to me when you could've come clean." After the week that's passed, I've only ever wanted the truth. "You knew where I was for months." I look at Ash. "And you didn't come to me, sit me down, and talk to me. You paid me to get naked for you, Ash."

He nods, and I wonder if he understands how painful this is for me. When those blue eyes meet mine, he admits, "I didn't want to hurt you."

"But you did," I tell him. My heart aches. My mind is whirling with all the information I've learned tonight. I need time to allow it to sink in. Somehow. "Take me home, Ember," I speak, but I don't recognize my voice.

"Sweetheart—"

"I said take me home," I bite out. I don't know who I'm angry at—Ash and Ember, their father, or myself.

"Katerina." Ash's voice steals my attention, his gaze locked on mine. Questions hang between us, unasked, unanswered.

"I'm going home." I turn and walk out of the kitchen, heading for the front door, and I wonder if I'll ever return. I hear the footsteps behind me, but I continue on, not wanting to look at Ash. As much as I'm angry at Ember, it's his brother who's hurt my heart because he's the one I've slowly been falling for.

Ember is behind the wheel as we weave through the streets. The moment he pulls up to the house, I thank him and get out of the car. I don't look back. I can't.

Once I'm in my bedroom, I curl up on my mattress and cry. I'm in the fetal position, holding onto my legs as if it will keep me from falling apart.

It won't.

It never can.

And in the depths of my tears, I wonder if I'll ever feel whole again.

ASH

IT'S BEEN TWO DAYS SINCE I TOLD HER THE TRUTH.
Forty-eight hours since she read the letters.

And one hundred and fifty minutes since she started going to class.

I know this because I've called the dean to *check on her* and he informed me she's been enjoying her subjects so far.

I've done all this because my little kitten hasn't wanted to talk to me. She asked for time. But I'm done with waiting. She's mine, and I'm going to get her back. I sent her a message earlier, telling her I'll be in the music room at the bar tonight. Nobody else knows that—only her, me, and the manager on duty. When I asked for the room to be cleaned and a bottle of whiskey to be waiting, he assured me everything would be in place.

I spent most of my childhood smiling, making sure

everyone was convinced that I was happy. But deep down, I knew I was different. Closing my eyes, I sigh, allowing my fingers to press on the keys, causing a deep, haunting sound to jump from the piano.

I lift my hands, then allow the featherlight touch of my fingertips to dance along the ebony and ivory, imagining it's Katerina's supple body. I want so much to stroke her, to feel her shudder and tremble under my touch.

It's been a long while since I paid for it since I wanted anyone but Katerina. Perhaps I should venture out again. Maybe it's best I don't touch my kitten because I know the moment I do, I'll never be able to walk away.

"That's pretty." Her sweet, serene tone comes from the doorway, but I don't look at her. My hands hover over the keys, and I wait. I'm not sure why, but I pray she tells me I'm wrong for her because I am. And even though I want her to walk away to keep herself safe, I'm coaxing her closer.

"It's from memory," I tell her, staring at the space where sheet music should be. "My mother taught it to me when I was just a child. I didn't even know what the different keys meant. All I knew were the melodies they made and how they fit together."

I feel her body beside mine on the small, black leather

bench. She's perched like a swan next to me, her back arched perfectly. She reminds me of the girls I watched up on stage when we visited the theatre.

"Can I play?" she asks with the innocence of a little girl.

I nod.

She smiles.

I want to kiss her.

How much restraint will it take not to pin her down right here and have my wicked way with her?

Apparently, all of it. Every ounce of me is needy for her. I'm throbbing in my dark slacks, and I'm thankful I decided to pull my shirt from the waistband, so it hangs loosely over my crotch.

Her fingers strum the keys, caressing and toying with them. I recognize the melody as a pop song by Halsey. If I'm not mistaken, she's playing "Heaven in Hiding" which I would never have thought could sound so good as a classical piece. But somehow it works.

"You lied to me." She speaks with her eyes closed and her fingers still dancing along each of the keys. "I don't like lies."

"I'm sorry, Kitten," I tell her. "I only wanted to keep you safe, make sure you were cared for by offering you an education and a home. But it was my mistake to hold back something like that from you."

"Safety doesn't come with lies. When you care about someone, you tell them the truth. Even if it may hurt them." She schools me gently, and I nod in agreement. I can't deny her. She's completely right.

Her gaze falls to the instrument. She doesn't look away from the keys while she plays, her body swaying side to side, and I can't help but envision her riding me with that same motion. When she finishes off the song, she turns to regard me. "Did you like it?"

"What?" I furrow my brows in confusion.

She smiles, leaning in, her mouth inches from mine. "The song."

"I'd love anything you played," I tell her honestly.

Her finger dances over one key, again and again, as if words are brewing in her mind, and she wants to let them out. I wish she'd tell me what she was thinking. I wish I could read her mind.

Suddenly, she's on her feet. I watch her sway in the silent room, dancing as if to a melody in her head. There's a playfulness about her. A light that shines when she spins around and around. Her feet fly across the floor, and I can't help but smile.

When she comes to a stop, she regards me. "I was so angry," she tells me.

"I know."

She shakes her head sadly. "I allowed my stupid emotions to get the better of me. I should've known better than to let myself to believe in something good."

"No, this is on me. I should've been the one to offer the truth to you," I admit, hoping she doesn't run again. "I care for you, Katerina."

"I want to fly away sometimes. I think about leaping off a cliff and soaring in the air." She sounds wistful as if this was something she could actually do, and it scares me. I can't lose her. I just can't.

"Have you been drinking, Kitten?" I tease, causing her to stop, her mouth pouting into a plump circle that doesn't help my erection calm itself.

"Did *you* tell the dean I was sorry for running out?" She questions suddenly.

"He understood it was too emotional for you," I tell her, nodding as I rise from my seat. I near her, but she spins away, her body moving like liquid flowing over rocks, fluid and pure.

"Do you really want to make it up to me?" she says, stopping inches from me.

"Of course I do. I would do anything for you." I almost drop to my knees, begging her to come to the house, to spend time with Ember and me. But I wait for her to speak.

"Take me on another date. Show me who you are."

My brows furrow in confusion. "What?"

"That's what normal people do. I want to be normal. Your father wanted me to experience life, and that's something I want." Kat shrugs.

Smiling, I respond, "I don't date."

"You fuck?" The word on her tongue is enough to have me groaning. The sound rumbles through my chest when she smiles. "Fuck."

"Katerina."

"Fuck."

"Kitten, I'm warning you."

She giggles playfully, and I'm enamored. "Fuck, fuck, fuck," she teases me, and I can't take any more.

Gripping her arm, I spin her around and plant her top half over the smooth black of the piano.

Her breasts are squashed against it, and her palms are flat, holding on. "What are you doing?"

I don't respond. I hitch up the skirt she's wearing and bunch it at her waist, finding soft blue cotton panties cupping her perfect little ass. Her pert cheeks are just begging for a spanking, and I deliver two hard blows to either one.

"Ouch!"

"Are you going to taunt me some more?" I question, holding her down so she can't move. "Kitten, answer me."

"Did anyone ever tell you that you're an asshole?"

"Yes, many times." I chuckle.

Her shy tone makes me want to rip off her panties and inhale her sweetness.

"Now, I'll ask you once more. Are you done teasing me?"

"Yes," she murmurs, and I release my hold on her. When she meets my gaze, her eyes are darker, almost a thundering gray. "Was that . . . did you like that?"

I nod. "Yes. Spanking you made my cock hard." I lean in closer to her before whispering my mouth over the smooth, supple flesh of her nape. "And if you'd continued to taunt me, I would've ripped your pretty panties off and fucked you hard against my piano." I step back, allowing her to really take in my promise. It's definitely not a matter of how, but a matter of when.

"You want me like that?" Her innocence shines through every word, and I watch her, confused at how she doesn't realize how much I really do crave her.

I turn away from her, not bothering to give her the response she wants. "I'll pick you up tomorrow afternoon at one. Be ready when I arrive."

"Wait! What do you mean?"

"You wanted a date?" I tell her. When I reach the door, I stop before turning to regard her and smile. "You'll get it."

After pushing through the exit, I step out of the room and signal my driver to wait for her. I'm tired, and I want to sleep. I'm also turned on and ready to fuck. But Kat's not there yet.

She's giving me a chance on her terms, and I'm going to do everything in my power to make her wishes come true.

She won't run away from me again.

Not now.

Not ever.

KATERINA

WHEN I WALKED INTO THE HOTEL BAR LAST night, I knew I was going to get Ash to agree to a date. My anger abated after I read the letters. I had time to think about what it meant to them to find me. I've reread each letter over and over until I came to the realization that their father only wanted what was best for them and me. And I decided to give them both a second chance.

Although, I'm still frustrated at both brothers for hiding things from me, I think everyone deserves a chance to make things right. Two days without Ash and I was missing him like I'd miss my next breath if it never came.

My phone rings startling me. Ember's name flashes on my screen, and I answer it before I have time to second-guess myself.

"Sweetheart," he greets, and I can hear the relief in

his voice.

"Ember, I wanted to call you. I saw Ash yesterday," I tell him in a rush.

"I know," he responds, and I can almost see the smile on his face in my mind's eye. "Thank you. Honestly, you didn't have to come back to us. We would've still paid your scholarship."

Shaking my head, I tell him, "This isn't about the money—well, not *only* about the money. I just . . . I missed him," I finally admit out loud, knowing that although it's dangerous, I have to allow myself to feel this.

"He missed you. I'm not trying to put any pressure on you, Kat, but . . . My brother needs you. He will need you."

Confusion arises at his words, and I question, "What do you mean?"

"I have to go. We'll speak soon." And then he's gone, leaving me frowning at my phone.

That was strange. Something doesn't feel right, but my stomach is in knots when I realize I need to finish my paper before tonight's date, so I let it go. For now.

I'll ask Ash what's going on with Ember.

He'll know.

The knock at the door makes my heart thud wildly. I wanted to be calmer when he arrived, but I'm still nervous about tonight. When I open the door, I'm met with Ash, who's dressed in a suit jacket and a light gray button-up that matches the clouds on a rainy day.

He isn't wearing a tie, and the first few buttons of his shirt are undone. Looking like a model, he saunters through the doorway, then cups my cheeks in his hands. "I've been thinking about this for hours."

I'm about to ask what, but his mouth lands on mine in a heated kiss. It's not as urgent and fiery as I expected; it's gentle and sensual.

Ash finally pulls away, leaving me breathless. He steps back and takes in my outfit. The sleek red dress is nothing like the one he got me for the gala, but it's exquisite, nonetheless.

"You look beautiful."

"Thank you," I tell him, grabbing my purse before I lock the door. He offers me his arm, which I accept, and for a moment, I forget about the pain of the past couple of days.

Ash is the perfect gentleman, opening the car door and helping me into my seat, and when he joins me, he turns on the heating without a word.

The drive is silent, and I wonder if he's going to speak, but he doesn't. All the way to a restaurant, we sit in the quiet, and I mull over what is going to happen tonight.

When we reach the small parking area, I'm confused as to where we're going. There's not much out here, and the number of small amount cars parked in the lot makes the place seem almost eerie. "What is this?"

Ash smiles when I turn to him. "It's a place that serves delicious food, delectable wine, and where we can talk," he tells me before exiting the vehicle and rounding the front. Pulling open my door, he offers me his hand, which I accept.

I realize as we head toward the building with a small red lit-up name above the door that, being an Addington, it's probably a place he owns. Once inside, the hostess takes us through the restaurant, which only has a handful of tables with patrons seated at them. We step down into a theatre-like space where there's a stage, along with a piano and a few tables surrounding the open area.

We're seated in a booth to the left of the stage, and the moment we're comfortable, I take note of the couples at each of the other tables who are all older than us and dressed impeccably. My gaze drifts over the elegant décor, understated with black everywhere. There are tufts of color—a deep crimson—which comes from the cushions on the bench seats, but other than that, it feels like everyone is hidden.

Lights overhead flicker, and when they're turned off, we're left in candlelight and the emergency lights, which offer a soft yellow glow. It's strangely romantic.

"I thought you didn't go on dates?" I question, picking up a menu.

Ash smiles. "I don't. This is one of my favorite places because I'm able to sit back, listen to music, and enjoy a meal."

"And how many girls have you brought here?" I tease, grinning like a lunatic. I'm allowed to; this is my second official date. I'm a woman who has a sort of normal life now. Shaking my head at the silliness, I watch Ash for his answer.

"I haven't brought anyone here. This, beyond my music room, is my sanctuary." He doesn't seem like he's lying. *What's going through his mind?* He looks so broken, so destroyed by what life has thrown his way, and I finally see myself in him.

I am him.

He is me.

Ember said Ash will need me, and it seems Ember is

the one who has taken our shards and fit them together.

Is this something he wanted to happen?

Did Ember plan for me and his brother to date? To be in a relationship?

No. He couldn't have known we'd be attracted to each other. But then again, Ember knew about me, my past.

"Is Ember okay?"

Ash starts at my question, furrowing his brows. "What do you mean?"

"He called me earlier, and he seemed . . . I don't know like something was wrong."

The waitress appears with a bottle of wine. I watch her uncork it with a flourish, then pour a taste for Ash. He takes a sip, then nods his approval.

She smiles politely as she pours the drinks, but I notice how she eyes Ash.

Soon after, we're alone, and his blue eyes pierce me.

"He seemed okay this morning, but then I only saw him for a few minutes because I had to go to the office."

I *clink* my glass on his before saying, "Okay, I just . . . I got a strange vibe from him." This time I'm watching Ash, and the expression on his face tells me he's worried.

"I'll talk to him when I get home tonight," he tells me, and I nod. "Tell me about your classes so far?"

"They're good. I'm excited to be doing a double major, but I'm not sure I can actually go through with it." It's the first time I've uttered those words. My father always taught me to be positive, to focus on what I can do, and even if I don't achieve it, I'll know I've tried my best.

"You will. Any help you need, tell me."

"I'd like to know more about your father," I say, before sipping my wine as I regard him. The shift in the air surrounding us is evidence that he's not comfortable with that topic, but I need to know. "Why didn't you give me the letters when we first met?"

"I was scared," Ash admits with a shrug. "I thought you would run a mile if you knew." He grips the wine glass so tight I wait for it to shatter into a million pieces. The pain on his handsome face makes me even more curious.

"What would've changed in your life if I had run?" I question gently.

"I wouldn't be here, now, with you." His admission makes my heart thud against my rib cage. "I like you, Kat."

"If this is going to work, there can't be any more lies, or secrets."

He's about to respond when the music starts. The melody is soft at first, just mere tinkling in the silence of the club. I glance behind me, taking in the man at the piano.

266

He's older, probably in his forties. He smiles at the other couples at their tables and plays a song I don't recognize.

Ash leans in his mouth at my ear. "I will promise you anything you want; just don't run."

The waitress places our entrees down, and I can't help but smile when I notice the plates laden with a delicious salmon salad, creamy dressing, and lemon drizzled on the top. The scent and flavors of the meal are out of this world. The opulence we're surrounded by is surreal and overwhelming. I thought I would feel out of place the moment we walked in, but I find myself relaxing into the evening and enjoying my second real date with Ash Addington.

EMBER

SHOVING THE OFFICE DOOR OPEN, I FIND MY brother perched behind his desk. I hardly come to Addington's offices, but today, I know we need to talk. It's time I told him what's going on and why he needs to make sure Kat is looked after.

"Brother." Ash smiles. "I wanted to ask you something last night after my date with Kat, but you were asleep."

It's true. I've hidden in the darkness each night. Painkillers no longer help.

"I was tired," I tell him, settling in the chair opposite the large desk my father insisted on having in his office. Even though I hate it now, as a kid, I loved sitting behind there, acting as if I were the CEO. When you're that small, everything seems exciting.

"Kat is slowly coming to terms with our admission," he tells me, and I realize he must've confessed his feelings toward her as well.

"Listen, there's something—"

The door flies open, and Larson comes strolling in as if he owns the fucking place. The man worked for my father for years, but I've never liked him, and I have a feeling the shit that caught up to my dad was because of him.

"Ashton, we need to talk about Los Angeles," he grunts out through huffed breaths. It's like he's run up the stairs or something.

"What's the problem?" Ash questions, leaning back in the large leather chair. His blue eyes gleam with mischief, and I'm confident someone's going home tonight without a paycheck.

"I think you're making a mistake. This is our livelihood and—"

"Our livelihood?" Ash pushes his seat forward. He's not happy.

"This company has been part of my life, and I'm not happy to stand by and watch a little kid run it into the ground. This isn't a playground," the older man utters in anger. It's like watching an intense tennis match. Ashton will not take this lightly.

My brother leans his elbows on the table, tugging

the chair closer to the desk. His shoulders are squared, his body rigid with tension. The air has turned thick and heavy. "You may have worked for my father, but other than being an employee, you have nothing to do with this company. And your livelihood . . ." Ash pauses, before biting out, "is in no way connected to Addington and Associates." His voice is laced with rage, and he's going to lose his shit with one of my father's oldest workers. "You may get a paycheck, but that's all it is."

"All I meant was—"

"And this is where you shouldn't *mean* anything." I rise, picking up the conversation in an attempt to calm Ashton down—he's ready to kill the asshole. "You're not running the company. If Ashton feels the decision is right, then I trust he knows what he's doing."

"I've been working here for over fifteen years, and your father would've wanted to open in Miami the moment he could . . ." His words trickle into nothing, and I can't help but smile. This asshole thinks he knows what he's doing, but Ash has already set up a meeting with the board members to inform them of the hold we're placing on purchase. Frederik won't win this war.

He rises, shoving the chair backward in anger. "This isn't over, Addington," he grits out through clenched teeth. "Your father wanted—"

This time Ash is on his feet, his body trembling with rage, and the blue in his eyes is darkening considerably. I've never seen him this angry before.

"You have no idea what my father wanted." His voice is ice cold, fanning the flames from Larson's attack. The older man simmers as he watches Ashton round the desk. "If you ever come in here again and throw around your supposed authority that has no ground in my office, in my company, I'll ensure you're on the street. Am I clear?"

"I want the best for this company. Buying the hotel in Miami would only benefit us."

The man doesn't give up. He would if he knew what was best for his future in this company. He needs to walk out. Ash has been running the company expertly since our father died. He knows what he's doing, having trained for this day most of his life. Yes, perhaps we're in an excellent place to buy in Miami, but we do need to focus on the properties we already have, bringing them up to par with our competition. Even I know that.

"You're welcome to take your shit and leave if you don't like how I run my company." Ash leans against the edge of his desk, waiting for Frederik Larson to make his choice.

With a nod, the older man turns and walks out the door without an apology.

I turn to my brother. His face is rigid, his jaw ticking with frustration.

"You know he's just a dick, right?" I question, watching him for any lingering doubts.

When Ash stepped up to take over, he wasn't sure if he was ready. There was always doubt in his mind that he could do it. But I know my brother. He's strong, and he has a good head on his shoulders.

"What's going on with you, Ember?" Ash asks, casting his gaze over me. "Kat mentioned she spoke to you, and you seemed *off*."

"There is something we need to talk about, but I didn't have the energy to do it last night." My voice cracks on the last word, which Ash will notice it.

"You're hiding things from me. I want to know what it is." His accusation is clear.

We always promised to be honest with each other. But I haven't been able to talk to him about this. Yesterday I got the confirmation I'd been dreading, and I knew I had to come here today and confess.

My conversation with Kat lingers in my mind. Secrets—they're the most destructive force when it comes to the people you love. I should be honest, I know it right down to my soul, but I can't bring myself to utter the words.

"If you wanted Kat—"

"That's not it," I tell him. "I care for her, yes, but she's yours. She always will be. I see how the two of you are together."

He doesn't respond, just shrugs and seats himself back in the chair.

My eyes burn with emotion. I don't want to admit this now. I came here to do it, and now I'm chickening out. Perhaps this is best done at home.

"I have to go. I'm making dinner for us," I tell him, rising from the chair. Instead, my lungs seize, and I can't help the onslaught of the cough that attacks me.

"You okay, brother?" Ash is at my side, his hands on me, holding me steady.

I cover it with a chuckle, swallowing back the bile that's burning in my throat, and I nod. "Yeah." I wave off his concern with a smile. "I'll see you later." I push by him, but I can feel the heat of his unwavering gaze on me. He doesn't believe me, and I know my lie was weak. "I'll speak to you tonight."

Once I'm in my car, I make my way home, hoping that

I'll have the courage to tell him. My brother will break. This news will shake his entire world, and I pray Katerina will be there to hold him.

Secrets.

They hold you in their feral grip, and once they're ready, they burn you to the ground.

ASH

FTER SHOVING THE DOOR OPEN, I STEP INTO THE house, which is silent. The spicy scent of dinner assaults me as I near the kitchen. It's empty. I continue through the house. *Where can Ember be?*

The first place I search is the studio, but that is empty as well.

I head to the music room. The door is ajar, and a faint melody trickles into the hallway. Kat was supposed to join us for dinner, but she hasn't let me know if she's running late. I'll call her once I talk to Ember.

He's sitting at the piano, his gaze locked on the instrument, but he doesn't notice me walk inside. I shut the door quietly and take my brother in. He seems as if he's lost in thought. He's always been jumpy, so if I startle him, he'll leap off the chair. I remember when we were kids, I would always do that, and it would make me chuckle.

"Em?" I call, keeping my voice low. When he turns to me, the pain in his expression steals all the air from my lungs. "What's wrong?"

"Kat is with Isobel this evening; they're having a girl's night, and . . ." He shakes his head as if she's gone for good. But that's not what he said.

"What happened, brother?" My voice is laced with fear, with worry. There's something else wrong, and I'm sure it's terrible because I've never seen him like this before. "Ember."

"I'm sick."

Out of all the things he could've said, that was not what I was expecting. It wasn't an admission I was prepared for. "What?" The word falls from my lips, grating against my throat as it echoes in the room.

"When I came to the office earlier, I wanted to tell you. Every night, I've wanted to pull you aside and just tell you." His words slice through my heart with the ferocity of a raging inferno.

"I don't understand. You're fine." A dark chuckle falls from my mouth, but it's humorless. There's pain etching itself onto every fiber of my being.

"The cancer's at stage four." He swallows, and I notice his agony from that motion alone.

It's then that it hits me—every evening we've had dinner together, I didn't notice Ember not eating—solids at least. He would have soup when I had steak or pasta. Anything substantial, he'd shove aside and tell me he'd had his fill.

"But I don't understand."

"I started getting dizzy at first. My vision would blur, and each day, it got worse. I put it off as nothing. As a headache," he whispers. "I didn't want to admit something was wrong."

My heart thuds painfully in my throat, attempting to choke me with emotion. It's a pain that sluices through me, reminding me that he's still talking, and this is real.

"They thought they could treat it, but it's a grade-four tumor," he tells me as he presses a key on the piano, causing the room to fill with a dark, dreadful sound. When he lifts his finger, he hovers both hands over the keys and allows his digits to flit over them, playing "Für Elise." It was the one song I taught him to play, the one song he'd wanted to learn.

I feel numb.

"What about surgery, chemo? There are new ways of treating this. I know there has to be. This isn't a fucking end, Ember. You will not leave me." My voice is filled with agony. A dark, brooding violence lances my chest, and I find it hard to breathe.

He shakes his head sadly, and tears trickle down his cheeks. "It's too late. I'll be going to the hospice tomorrow. It's time, Ash."

I want to punch something, to break something, to rip something to pieces, just like my heart is shattering. I've never been one to show emotion. I hate allowing people to see me at my most vulnerable, and right now, I'm more broken than I have ever before. Losing my father was difficult, but that doesn't compare to this. Not even in the slightest.

When Ember finishes the song moments later, I fall to my knees beside him. For the first time in my life, I break completely. I sob. Looking at the brother who's lived only a quarter of his life, I don't know how much longer he has.

He rises and turning toward me, finally meeting my pained stare with a warm one of his own. I push to my feet, finding my knees buckling at the heaviness that's hanging on my shoulders.

"I'm ready, Ash. You just need to take care of Kat." He places a hand on my shoulder, much like a father would to a son. I want to shake him off, to tell him he's full of shit and he's not going anywhere. But I can't.

I pull him into an embrace. I blink and a torrent streams down my face. My body shakes and his shivers. There's agony gripping me in a fierce hold, and I know there's no way I'll be able to move on from this.

I don't know how long we stand there, but when I finally move away, Ember nods, and leaves me in the place I always found solace. But this time, there's none of that to be had, because right now, this room is a reminder of how alone I am.

"Hi." Kat's sweet voice stirs me from sleep, and I blink my eyes open to find her perched on the foot of my bed. She's wearing a pair of shorts that look far too small for her, and a loose-fitting white top that hides her pretty tits.

"What are you—"

"Ember had to go somewhere. He said to wake you before ten and tell you to take me out somewhere nice," she informs me with a smile. "He's been acting rather strange lately. Do you think he has a girlfriend?"

Her question is innocent enough, but I find my throat closing at the memory of my brother's confession. She doesn't know. Of course, he's going to leave the difficult part to me.

"No, he's . . . There's just a lot going on," I tell her. Pushing off the bed, I turn to regard her, noticing how her gaze trails over my bare chest down to my boxers, and my very obvious morning hard-on.

"I . . . um . . . I guess I'll wait in the kitchen." She stumbles over her words, which make me smile.

And I now realize what my brother did. He was toying with Kat and me, pushing us together in his own way.

"You're not shy, are you?" I smile, stepping closer to her, craving normalcy in this shit-show world of mine. "Kitten," I coo, cupping her face in my palm, allowing my thumb to swipe along the apple of her cheek that's turned pink. "Tell me."

"Of course not," she huffs, squaring her shoulders. She looks like a kitten wanting to swat at a toy. Cute, sweet, and playful.

I lean in, eating up the few inches between our faces, and plant my lips on hers. It's a chaste kiss, soft and filled with promise. I don't open my mouth. I don't deepen it. I only offer her a lingering brush of my lips.

Her breaths are uneven. They become more ragged, the longer we stay in this position. Things are becoming serious between us, more so than I'd imagined, and I need to share everything with her today.

There can't be any secrets between us. Or this will never work.

"We'll go for a picnic," I whisper along her cheek, hoping the fresh air will take away the sting of what I need to do. I hate that he's left me to do this. But Ember knows I'd do anything for him. "We have lots to talk about." My words flutter over her ear, and she trembles. "Wait in the kitchen. I'll be out in twenty minutes." I step back, noticing her cheeks have flushed a deep pink. I watch her turn and walk out of the room before I grab my cell phone from the nightstand. I hit call on my brother's number and press the phone to my ear.

"Ash," his voice is raspy as if he's been screaming.

It's only your imagination. He needs you to keep it together.

"I know you're not here; I'm taking her to the picnic spot, and I'm going to tell her everything."

"I didn't say goodbye to her." He sounds sleepy, could be the medication. *He hasn't even told me if they've put him on anything that could help.*

Shaking my head, I run my fingers through my hair in frustration. "I can't believe you just left this morning. I need time, Ember. You can't—"

"Visiting hours are six to nine. Come by, and we'll talk

some more. I love you, brother." He hangs up before I can respond, and I fling the phone against the wall causing it to shatter in a million pieces. Just like my heart and soul.

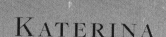

KATERINA

THE CAR IS SILENT. ASH HASN'T TURNED ON THE stereo, and when I asked where we were going, all he said was "out." I'm nervous about what's going on, but I've left him to stew in whatever is bothering him.

He makes a left off the main road, and we head through the high oak trees that I've seen from the mansion. They're stunning. We pull onto a dirt road which goes on for miles ahead of us. Ash abruptly turns off and cuts the engine. We sit for a moment before he glances at me, his expression is unreadable. Blue pierces through me looking right into the broken-hearted part of me.

"Thank you for coming out with me today," he finally utters. His voice is husky with emotion, raspy, and he clears his throat as if to ward off the pain laced in his tone.

"Are you going to tell me what's going on?" I question, watching for the hint of a negative response. But he only smiles. He pushes open the driver's door before exiting, leaving me in the car for a moment. He opens my door and helps me out.

He grabs the basket from the trunk and offers me his hand, which I gratefully accept. We walk in more silence. It weighs on me.

Is he going to tell me to leave?

Are they done with me, and now I'm meant to go back to work for Maria?

Does he no longer want me in his life?

I'm nervous.

I've only ever been this scared once before, and it was the moment I was ripped from my childhood home by the state and put into foster care.

We exit the thick forest into a clearing and before us is a lake. It's breathtaking.

"This is amazing." I sigh, walking toward the water, and Ash releases my hand, allowing me to venture farther. I glance behind me and watching Ash set down the basket, then pull out the blanket. He's thought of everything.

The sun is high in the sky now, which is bright blue while the water has taken on a dull navy, almost charcoal shade. I've never been somewhere so stunning before. With the trees surrounding the lake, it doesn't feel like we're merely forty minutes outside the city.

"Are you hungry?" Ash questions, his body right behind mine, while strong arms snake around my middle, and he tugs me back against him enveloping me completely.

"I didn't peg you for a romantic." I smile, taking in the view. It's the first time in a long while that I've truly felt at peace.

"I'm not, but I promised Ember I'd be nice. Normally I would've taken you to my bed, laid you down, and eaten your pretty pussy until you were gushing all over my face. Then, while you were still trembling, I'd slide into you and make you scream my name." He tells me honestly, with mischief dancing in his eyes, and the Ash I know is back. But it's only for a second before he's trying to make light of whatever's bothering him.

"You're always so vulgar," I sass. "So, why does Ember want you to be nice to me?" My question earns me a hard stare before he pulls me along to the blanket.

There's a fire licking at the edges of my happiness. I have a gut feeling a blaze is about to tear through everything I've come to care for over the past couple of weeks. Ash's mood has made me weary, and I turn in his arms to look at him directly. Hoping I can find the answers in his expression.

Once we're settled, Ash opens the basket and pulls out sandwiches and two bottles of chilled water. "When I was younger, Ember was always my sanity. I would run riot, and he would calm me down." He bites into his sandwich, staring out at the lake. His jaw works as he chews and his throat bob when he swallows. "I knew I'd always need him to be there, to be my foundation. He kept me grounded."

"He has a special way about him," I agree before biting into my bread roll.

"He does. Kindness follows him everywhere. Over the years, I've watched in awe as he's interacted with his students, our company employees, and even strangers with patience and genuine kindness. Our father was different. I take after him, whereas my brother is like my mom." He finishes his food, then opens the water to gulp down a couple of mouthfuls.

"You've lost a lot," I respond, swallowing past the lump of emotion that's threatening to choke me.

When Ash turns to me, those azure pools are shimmering with emotion. He blinks once, and a lone tear trickles down his cheek. *He's crying.*

I'm on my knees beside him in seconds, wrapping my arms around him, holding him to my chest. I close my eyes, questioning myself, *what has brought this on?*

I've seen Ash act like a complete asshole, and I've accepted it. I knew he was closed off but watching him break down right before me, is more than I can take.

He pulls away. Reaching for my face, he cups my cheeks, holding me steady before kissing me. It's not rushed, or hungry; it's like he's pouring his pain into me, and I swallow it without question.

If I can ease the heartache, I'll do it. Our tongues dance slowly, tangling and twining around each other. His lips are hot on mine, and I can feel his tears falling freely. Something is drastically wrong.

Pulling away, I look into his eyes, "Tell me what's wrong?"

He doesn't say anything for such a long time. I don't think he'll respond.

"My brother is dying," he croaks, choking on the words. And for the first time since we met, I see Ashton Addington completely shatter.

His torment, his pain, everything he's kept hidden spills free, and my heart breaks in two.

ASH

SHE HOLDS ME.

Her tears soak my shirt, and I know she's hurting too. They've grown close, and she's come to care for Ember.

I don't know how I'm meant to go on without him in my life.

"I'm so sorry," she mumbles into the material, causing the murmur to get lost. There's agony in every word, and for her to break like this, I know she's special. Ember was right all along—she is going to be the one to hold me together. "I'm so, so sorry."

Kat's arms are warm around me, and mine twine around her. Her small frame fits perfectly under my arms. We hold each other for so long, I don't notice the sun sinking between the trees. The sky has turned a fiery orange, and we'll soon be in the dark if we don't get a move on.

"We have to go," I tell her, remembering the visiting hours. "We need to go see him." I pull away, realizing I haven't yet told her the one other thing I wanted to when I brought her out here.

How much I care for her.

But I needed her to know about Ember before it was too late.

My heart feels heavy. I can't heal the pain in my chest, and I know nothing ever will, but Katerina eases it. She brings light to the darkest parts of my mind.

"Ash," she calls to me, causing me to meet her gaze. "I'd like to take you up on the second part of the offer. I'm not going anywhere." She doesn't have to explain.

"I don't expect you to live your life in the mansion. Your studies are paid for—there's no going back. I've signed the agreement."

"This has nothing to do with that," she responds with confidence. "This is something more." For the first time, she's the one closing the distance. "I've come to care for you both. And I want to be there for you." Her voice calms me like a balm.

"I can't . . . There's nothing I can offer you to make you happy," I assure her. It's true. I never thought I could make another person happy. As much as I may care for her, love her even, I want to see her happy, and I'm not sure that will be with me.

A forever is something I can never let myself have.

I'm too much like *him*.

My father was a cold man, frigid and distant, and I vowed to never bring anyone into my life and have them feel the loneliness I'm certain my mother felt. Both Ember and I certainly did.

"We aren't our parents." Her words still me for a moment.

I don't know how to respond. Perhaps she's right. But I've spent my life convinced that I've turned into the man who raised us. Even Ember's said it over the years.

"Let's go see Ember," I offer finally, unsure of what else to say.

Kat follows me to the car, and once we're seated, I turn on the engine and pull out onto the road. It's not dark yet, but the night is coming, the time I hate being alone. I turn on the stereo and the deep, melodic rap of NF filters through the speakers as he sings "Paralyzed."

"I like this song," Kat murmurs sadly. "I felt like that for a long time after my parents died." Her voice is distant, and I'm certain memories are plaguing her as much as they haunt me.

How can two broken souls go through so much, yet find themselves again?

Is there any hope for us?

I can't answer her because I'm not sure how to soothe her agony, so instead of speaking, I nod and watch the road before us.

It doesn't take long to reach the hospital, to park, and for us to comfortably fall into step beside each other as we make our way to the building. The moment we step foot inside the entrance, Kat's fingers twine through mine, her warm hand scorching me.

"I'm here to see Ember Addington," I tell the nurse.

She offers a solemn nod before tapping the keys on her computer. "Yes, he's on the third floor. Room 398C."

She doesn't tell me if he's okay or not, and my heart lurches into my throat, threatening to choke me.

Kat and I make our way to the elevator, and once inside, she turns to me, pinning me with those gray eyes. "Don't push me away," she pleads. She fucking begs.

How on earth can this girl ever think I'll be the one pushing her away?

She's given me more in the time I've known her than any woman has ever done in a lifetime of seeking solace in them.

My mouth opens, but no words come out. There's nothing I can say that will make this okay. I can't offer assurance—not right now when it feels as if I'm floating above the clouds, almost dream-like because none of this feels real. I pull her into a hug, holding her slender frame within my arms. She's so warm, it's like she's about to burst into flames.

The doors slide open, depositing us on the third floor with bright white linoleum that blinds me. Everything is sterile. It's too white, too clean, too sickly.

The numbers take us down the hall until we reach the large silver ones for Ember's ward. Kat steps forward, but I hold her back. I don't know if I can walk inside. I don't know if I can see my brother in there, breaking, getting weaker.

Swallowing and breathing become difficult the more I stare at the numbers. They start to blur. My lungs work harder to pull in air. When I glance down, blinking away the emotion, I see it—Katerina's hand on my chest, right where my heart is.

"We both need to walk in there and be strong for him." Her tone is low, her voice a whisper, but it sounds as if it's surrounding me. "When we get home, you can fall apart. But not here. Not in front of him."

Nodding, I swipe my hand at my face, making sure I'm respectable when I push open the door and tug her in behind me. Katerina is different. She's burrowed her way into my heart so deeply, and so permanently. I can't let her go.

EMBER

"**L**OOK WHAT THE CAT DRAGGED IN." I CHUCKLE, then fall into a bout of coughing which makes my throat burn. Ash has been crying. His lashes are wet but his hold on Kat's hand assures me he'll be okay.

They're perfect together. I knew they would be.

I knew how conflicted she was when I kissed her. I had to know if her heart was his. If they could only sort their shit out and admit how they felt about each other, I'd be happy.

"You're an asshole," the little kitten bites out. "Why didn't you tell me where you were going? Tell me what was going on?" She rushes to my side before leaning in and placing a kiss on my cheek.

I feel like shit, the chemo is literally nauseating, and the food here is a joke, but I can't help chuckling at her.

"If I told you, you may have killed me anyway," I

mumble into her ear causing her to playfully swat at me. But when she pulls away, her cheeks are wet. "Hey," I admonish. "None of that." I reach for her face, wiping my thumb along her cheek and pressing it to my lips. "Mmm, sweetness."

"What did they do today?" Kat questions, her voice cracking on the last word.

"They're just pumping my veins full of drugs. It's meant to make me *comfortable*, but it makes me feel worse. I can't do it." A cough wracks through me, causing me to splutter, and both Ash and Kat help me, holding me up. The pain shoots through every limb in my body, but I smile through it.

"How long have you known? I mean, how bad is it?" Kat's questions are the ones I was expecting from Ash, but he's silent. Watching, waiting.

Meeting Kat's gaze, I offer a sad smile. "The tumor is inoperable," I rasp, the emotion clogging up my words. I take a long inhale before continuing, "It's grown too much. And chemo won't cure it, it'll only prolong the inevitable."

I haven't said it out loud to anyone. Not even when the doctor went through the results.

"But I don't understand how this wasn't caught earlier. And I mean, you don't look like you're . . ." Kat's words taper into nothing, and I know what she wants to say. It's so clear on her pretty face. She has such a delicate way about her and seeing her right here, perhaps it's the drugs, but there's something ethereal about her.

"Kat, sweetheart," I whisper her name gently. "I knew for a while; I just couldn't bring myself to admit it. I didn't want to hurt anyone."

"You hurt me by not telling me." Ash perches on the bed, his hand holding mine like we used to do when we were children. "You were meant to confide in me."

"I wanted you to remember me the way I was. If I'd have told you months ago, you would've looked at me with pity, with fear, and that was something I couldn't bring myself to ever allow. I wanted you to see me, not cancer, not the tumor on my brain."

Ash shakes his head in frustration. "If it's this bad, how are you still—"

"So handsome?" I chuckle darkly. "The way it's been growing has slowly limited my movement; you didn't notice how I couldn't do certain things anymore. I would spend days inside when I felt weak when my body was at war with the disease. My vision would be blurred to a point where I couldn't read or paint anymore. It would come in waves, so I managed to hide it from you. The dizzy spells would hit me at times, but I never allowed you both to see it."

"When I was at the hotel," Ash mutters, and I nod.

Each night he went out allowed me to hide the pain. In the morning, I'd swallow meds to numb the agony coursing through my limbs. But it's time to stop fighting what's coming. "I can't be here forever, Ash," I tell him.

He shakes his head.

The sadness that emanates from my brother is like a fiery inferno, ready to ravage everything in its path. The destruction that I've caused by not telling him only seems to have made it worse. But given a choice, I'd do it again. It was what I needed.

"You have a life to create. My story is coming to an end." I never wanted him to know. I didn't want him living in the house with me, waiting for the moment when I didn't wake up.

"I don't like this. I fucking hate this whole fucked up story," Ash finally says, but his tone is filled with agony. He peers at me. Those pained blue eyes held so much *more* than I could have ever imagined.

The knock on the door comes too soon. I want more time to talk to them both, but I know in the morning they'll be back.

"We're not leaving," Ash says, rising from the bed. He stalks toward the nurse and has a long, hushed conversation while I grip Katerina's hand in mine. The medication is slowly starting to make me sleepy. I'll be of no use to them pretty soon.

I hate the feeling of numbness that overcomes me. I've always avoided any painkillers or cold medication. I've kept even alcohol to a minimum. But right now, I'd drink a bottle of bourbon with my brother just to take the edge off.

When Ash returns to the bed, he meets my gaze before informing me of his plans. "Kat and I will get a room across the road. The hotel is not bad, and we'll be back in the morning." He doesn't ask for Katerina's agreement in this, and I know she may bristle at the thought of having her choice taken away.

"Kat?" I turn to her. "Are you okay with that? You really don't have to—"

"I'll be here. It's Saturday tomorrow, so I don't have classes, and I would've stayed even if it weren't." She smiles down at me.

When she leans in and places a kiss on my cheek, I revel in her heat.

"Anything for you." Her words are a whisper, and I

298

don't think Ash heard.

"Tomorrow, brother." Ash's voice sounds unsure. I've never seen my brother so broken before. Not even when our dad died.

"I'll be here."

I settle back in my uncomfortable hospital bed once they leave. *How will Ash continue without me?* He's got a fiery woman on his hands, and I know she'll keep him busy. But he holds so much inside. Sadness hits me, along with another bout of coughing, and I press the button for the nurse.

He'll have to come clean and admit he loves her. I know he's never said that to anyone outside our family before. But he'll have to make his choice—either swallow his pride and convince her to stay with him or decide to let her go and allow her to live her life without him.

By then, I'll be gone.

KATERINA

THE COUCH IS COMFORTABLE.

I'm sitting alone, a glass of wine in hand, but my heart hurts. I haven't known Ember for long, but it feels as if he's been here my whole life. We have a connection of sorts. One that's unique. A true friendship.

I blink, and the tears fall once more. They don't want to stop, and I don't know how to make them go away. It sucks having non-stop tears again, but it's the only way to know this is real.

The knowledge that someone you care for, someone you love, is no longer going to be around is painful to come to terms with.

Seeing him today hurt me. And I can't imagine what Ash is feeling.

He's perched on a chair on the balcony. A call from work came through, and as far as I can tell he's trying to put out a fire with the staff member.

He's not himself.

Anger and rage are slowly consuming him like a fire waging war on his heart, and I don't know if I'll be able to calm it down. Ember believes I can. I know he does. But I have never had the confidence in myself to perform miracles.

"Sorry about that," Ash says, stalking into the room. He flops on the sofa and pulls me onto his lap. "I wasn't sure how this would work," he tells me absentmindedly. "You and I . . . I don't know how to describe it."

"If you don't want—"

"Don't get me wrong," he continues, ignoring me. "I want you. I want this," he says as he waves a hand between us. "And my brother knew I would." The confidence in his tone is pure. It soothes my fears, my worry that he may just send me away.

His hands hold my hips, gripping them tightly, and then he moves them, back and forth. It's a gentle yet commanding motion and my core rubs against his bulge.

"Are you sure?" I question, my hands landing on his shoulders, holding on tight.

His gaze is filled with fire; flames of desire dance wildly within them. "Make me think of nothing else but you," he tells me.

I move of my own accord. Leaning in, I steal his mouth with mine. Our lips mold together, and our tongues dance and tangle as pleasure zings through me. Every nerve in my body is alight with need. I'm wet.

If he put his fingers inside my panties, he'd find my arousal for him. His firm hands grip my ass, pulling me tighter against him. My fingers tangle in his hair, and the heat between us is unbearable.

Ash seems to notice and tugs at my clothes.

I fumble at his waistband, pulling at his shirt and the moment it's on the floor, my fingertips trail over his taut, toned flesh. Dips and peaks of smooth tanned skin greet me. There aren't any blemishes. *How can he be this perfect?*

His mouth moves from mine, over my cheek and down to my neck. He suckles the sensitive skin before grazing it with his teeth and causing me to shiver with anticipation.

I'm in a bra and panties by the time he's lifted me and walked us into the bedroom.

After laying me down, he hovers over me for a moment, then settles between my thighs. The buckle of his belt taunts my clit, and when he elicits a whimper from me, the wolfish smirk on his lips reveals he's about to torture me some more.

He moves in slow, steady thrusts, rubbing the smooth metal over my mound. My hips rise, but he pins them back down, holding me hostage.

"I've wanted this for so long." He breaks the silence. His voice is raspy, low, and gravelly. His eyes have turned dark with lust.

I reach behind me, and unclasp my bra, allowing it to fall on the mattress.

Ash's gaze darkens further, and his mouth descends on my nipple. Suckling the bud into his mouth, he bites down hard enough to draw a mewl from my lips. He releases the tortured peak, then moves to the other. Repeating the action, he licks and sucks me until my body is trembling.

"Are you going to come, Kitten? Will you purr for me?" His taunts are only fuel to the fire already raging inside me. Ash trails his mouth down my body, over my stomach, and even lower still. He pulls my panties along with his motion and soon, I'm bared for him.

"Please, Ash, just do it?"

My begging only makes him chuckle.

"I'm taking my time with you, Kitten," he tells me. Then, his mouth is on me. I feel the warmth of him suckling me, licking me. His tongue dips into my pussy, and I can't help but cry out from the pleasure exploding inside me.

He sucks my clit into his mouth, then pumps two fingers into me, easing them in and out in a torturously slow motion which has me tugging at his hair. I want him closer, farther away, closer. I don't even know. His assault on my body is pure bliss.

"So fucking delicious," he growls against my wet entrance. "Will you come for me?"

I can't find words, so I nod. Of course, I will. How is that even—my thoughts are halted when Ash inserts a third finger, then grazes the throbbing nub with his teeth, which sends me over the edge, and I'm crying out the only word I can think of at that moment—his name.

I don't know how long I lie there. But when I open my eyes, Ash is between my legs once more. Only this time, he's naked along with me, and his cock is pushing against my pussy.

"I want to go slow," he tells me, inching forward. He groans when he's inside me. "Fuck."

"Please, just move," I beg again. He's brought me to the precipice and pushed me over, and now I'm nearing that same place once more.

His hips roll, pushing forward, and his cock spears

into me, inch by inch.

"If I move any faster, you'll break in two, Kitten." He smiles down at me. His hands are on either side of my head as if he's cocooning me in his affection. I want to say, love. I want to believe love. And I do. In this moment, with just our bodies locked together, I *feel* the love.

"What if I want you to break me in two?" I challenge with a soft laugh that makes him offer me *that* smile. The one that I've wanted to see on his face every day since we met.

Without warning, he plunges into me, fully seating himself, knocking the breath from my lungs.

My nails dig into his shoulders, and my legs wrap around his taut waist, pulling him impossibly deeper.

"You're so fucking tight; too perfect for my cock." His tone is reverent. His words bathe me in love. I can say it because that's what it is.

He pulls out, almost all the way, then glides back in. I'm so wet. He doesn't seem to care, though. He's lost in pleasure, and he takes me along with him.

We move in sync. As if we were made to be together, to fit with each other. The feel of his thickness opening me, my body molding to his, and accepting him deeply— it's as if he's drawing out my pleasure, my heart, and my soul all at the same time.

My back arches the moment he moves faster, hitting the spot inside me that has my toes curling and my nails nearly breaking the skin.

"Little kitty has claws." He smiles, peppering kisses all over my face. His hips slam me into the mattress, and I'm lost to the electric pleasure zipping through every inch of me.

"Ash, Ash, oh God," I mumble as my head falls back and my body shakes and trembles, pressed against his.

He tugs my nipple into his mouth before biting down on the pebbled bud, causing my body to spasm as I scream his name so loudly, I'm sure everyone in the hotel will hear.

"God, your pretty pussy feels good milking my cock, Kitten," he growls, and I feel him thicken, opening me even more. And then heat fills me, over and over again, until his body stills above mine.

I open my eyes and look directly into those darkened blue pools, and even though they're filled with calm affection, I'm burnt from the inside out.

I've fallen.

I've walked right into the inferno.

And there's no escape for me now.

ASH

TWO DAYS HAVE PASSED SINCE THE FIRST TIME Kat, and I visited Ember in hospital. And even though I didn't think it was possible, I've only become more attached to Katerina.

My heart hurts the most at night when I think of losing my brother. But having her body curled against mine offers me solace.

Love is an emotion that guts you when you're least expecting it. And even though it scares me more than I thought, I'm taking a leap with Kat, and I no longer doubt it. After feeling her around me, her warmth, and her pleasure, I'm a man addicted.

"You know," Ember tells me, "I think you're in love, but you're too afraid to admit it." My brother grins, and even though it makes me smile, the sadness in my heart is ever present.

He's getting weaker each day. His face is hollow, the dark circles under his eyes are more prominent, and I fear it won't be long now. I can't bear to see him like this, to watch him wither away, but I have to be here. I need to be.

"Perhaps I am, brother," I admit. "But how can I know for sure if she loves me?"

His green eyes aren't as bright as they used to be. He's not going to be beside me forever, not like we'd always promised each other.

"Real love isn't about fear; it's about trusting in each other. I understand you're worried she'll decide it's merely a passing phase, but you have to take a chance. Or you'll regret it forever."

"How can you be so sure?" Ember has always been an old soul. Far more mature than me, he would be the one to offer advice even when I didn't take it, and I knew he was right.

"Do you remember what Mom told us about when she met Dad?" He questions, but before I can respond, he continues. "They had split for two long years before she finally relented and gave him an ultimatum; no more partying if he wanted her."

I nod. "Yeah, I remember. And the bastard did stop." I chuckle, recalling the night. We were still quite young. It's strange how you can remember things that happened so long ago.

"Katerina is yours; she was made for you," Ember insists, squeezing my hand. His fingers are bony. His body is slowly giving up. I'm not sure how much longer I'll have my brother with me, but I've spent every day here with him, talking about the times we were young and carefree. "I hate you for leaving me."

"You don't hate me; you're just angry," he responds with clarity. "When we lose people we love, we get mad, and *you* tend to go off the rails at times. Remember that in the future, when you and Kat have a fight. Give her time."

"How do you know I'll stay true to her?"

"Because you're my twin. I know everything there is to know about your sorry ass," he bites out, but it's no longer filled with fire. His flames are dimming, and I don't know if I can bear to watch them flicker out.

"You're an asshole, brother." I smile. "I love you."

"I love you too," he tells me, and I notice the shimmer of emotion on his lashes. He looks just like our mother. "Now, go to your girl. And remember what I said."

"You better be here tomorrow to make sure she's not scared off by my stupid admission," I warn him before planting a kiss on his forehead. It's so clammy. I close my eyes for a moment, and for the first time in my life, I pray. I don't know who can hear me, but I ask for a little more time. Just a bit more.

"You know it."

After I leave the hospital, I drive in silence through the dark roads. I dropped Kat at home earlier because she had homework to complete, and she's studying for a test. I want to take her somewhere special tonight, and I hope she's finished up all her work.

If I'm finally going to utter those three words properly—not us arguing, or her being angry at me, I want it to be perfect.

And I know it will be.

I shut the door behind me and make my way through the house into the living room. I find Kat sitting on the sofa, a pen twirling in her mouth, and her hair pinned in a messy bun. She's the epitome of innocence.

"Hey," I call, before settling myself behind her.

Her gray eyes meet mine, and they're bloodshot. "How is Ember? Did he say anything?" she questions. Setting the book down, she bites on the end of the pen as she regards me.

"He said I should take you out this evening," I inform her with a smile.

"Oh?" She offers me a small grin, but it doesn't reach her eyes. I know she's worried about him. I am too. I wish it were easier. I wish with everything I have that he could come home, but I know it's futile.

I pull her into my arms and, like we do each night, we sit in silence. The only sounds are the sobs from Kat. I blink back my tears. I need to be strong, even though I don't feel it. Pressing a kiss to the top of her head, I hold her close.

"There's something I need to say," I tell her.

Kat shifts so she's on my lap. Her hands grip my shirt, and she watches me with wide, doe eyes. "Please don't tell me it's something bad."

"I love you." The words fall with ease from my lips, and her mouth drops open in surprise. I can't believe I just blurted that shit out. It was meant to be special. I've fucked it up again.

"Ash, I—"

The shrill ringing of my cell phone interrupts her, and I pull it from my pocket. The number on screen makes my heart lurch in my chest.

"Mr. Addington," the doctor utters, "I think it's best you come to the hospital."

KATERINA

EMBER DOESN'T LOOK WELL. HIS BODY IS FIGHTING a losing battle, and so is my heart.

When I first met them, I didn't know if I could ever choose between the two men who sauntered into my life and offered me everything I'd ever wanted. Now I'm watching, through the thick pane of glass, from a distance, as an outsider.

As if he can feel my eyes on him, Ash turns to regard me. He looks like he hasn't slept in days, weeks even. He rises, giving his brother a kiss on the forehead before he turns and makes his way to the door.

The moment Ash steps out of the room to where I wait in the corridor, I fall into his arms. I don't know where they come from, but tears trickle down my cheeks. The emotions I've been holding onto in these past few hours are breaking free, and I can't stop them.

Ash's arms are warm, cocooning me, but this time, they can't stop the pain. His affectionate hold is all that's keeping me from falling to the ground.

"I'm so sorry," I mumble into his shirt. I've soaked the material. I know he doesn't mind, but I do so I pull away. "I'm—"

"You shouldn't be sorry. There was no way of telling with how Ember is," he says. "I think he'd be glad to see you if you'd like to come inside." Ashton leans in close, pressing his lips to the top of my head.

"I'd like that a lot," I tell him honestly.

He pulls me in, allowing me to enter the dimly lit room which is so big, there's a seating section where Ash guides me toward. They've reserved visitation rights only for family, but Ash has tugged me along anyway. Ember is sleeping, his eyes closed, and I can't stop the tears from falling. He seems blurry through the pain that's lacing my heart.

I may not have known him for long, but I feel as if he was a part of me. I guess they both are in a way. Perhaps not family, but they mean something to me.

Love is strange. It creeps up on you, weaseling its way through the darkness, bathing you in light, giving you hope.

Pain is real. It has been the only thing I've known since I was sixteen, and I realized that it could so easily kill you if you let it.

"He asked for you a few times," Ash tells me. "They've just made him comfortable now," he murmurs, settling beside me on the couch that faces the rest of Ember's room.

"I'll go in to see him in a minute. I wanted to say something to you earlier," I whisper, looking into those beautiful blue eyes. "I love you, Ash." I don't wait for a response but make my way to the bed.

The moment I settle in the chair, I reach for Ember. His fingers tighten around mine, causing me to glance at him. He blinks twice; perhaps a thank you, or a hello. My throat constricts with emotion as I watch him. It's strange to see someone *disappear* before your very eyes.

I swallow past the lump that's making it difficult to breathe when his eyes close again, and I know it's the last time I'll ever see those green pools.

Ash shakes his head, his gaze locked on his brother's frail body on the hospital bed.

His skin is sallow, and I wonder if there could've been a better chance for treatment if he'd tried something sooner. "Did he ever tell you how long he knew before this

. . .?"

Ash is silent for a long while, and I wonder if he's going to respond, but I don't press him for more information. I just stare at a man who buried himself in my heart without me realizing it.

"No. Stubborn bastard." The words are grit out through clenched teeth, but I know he's in pain.

"What else did my father say?" Ash questions suddenly, and I realize he is talking about the letter.

"Just that he loved you both so much. He tried to help me because he felt guilty for not being able to go back in." I glance at Ash's hand and slip mine into it. Our fingers twine together. "He also told me to look out for you both."

"He can be such an asshole sometimes. He shouldn't have put that on you. If you need to move out, to put space between—"

"Why didn't you just tell me who you were from the beginning?"

He stares into nothingness when he responds, "How would you have reacted if I told you?"

"So, making me fall in love with you was better than the truth," I say with a deadpan expression and an arched brow. He pulls my hand up to his mouth and presses a kiss to it.

We sit in silence, watching Ember sleep. And as I lean into Ash, I blink back the tears.

ASH

'YOU'RE AN ASSHOLE IF YOU WALK AWAY from her now.' He writes on the notebook I brought with me. He stopped talking when they inserted the tube into his esophagus. At first, he didn't want it, but they explained it would be the only way to feed him. When he could no longer swallow anything, it required an emergency surgery; they operated.

The way his throat bobs when he attempts to swallow makes me want to help him. To do something other than watch my brother die.

My chest is tight with the heartache that's slowly eating at me. I want to turn away, to focus on something other than his frail body. He's too young for this bullshit. He's not even been in love, or gotten married, or had a family, for God's sake. And he never will.

"I love her, Ember," I confess quietly. "I'll ask her, but

not now. We need time to get over this. To ... I don't know
..."

'*My brother is a chicken.*' This time, he smiles when he writes the words down. It's nothing like the smiles he used to offer up when he wanted to get his own way, but it's a grin nonetheless. Even in pain, in the last few days, I have with him, he's smiling.

I nod. It's true. When it comes to Katerina Nielsen, I've never been more fearful in my life. The thought of losing her makes me ache. It makes the pain from losing Ember just that much worse.

"You knew. All this time, you watched me walk down the path into her arms. All those nights we spent looking for her, trying to find her. You knew I would fall for her."

He nods slowly and winces before he grabs my hand. He takes the pen and scrawls messily on the page. When I glance down, there are only two words. My throat closes as emotion chokes me. All our lives we've dealt with death, with lies and secrets, but we've always been there for each other.

And soon, I'll have to go it alone. There will only be one Addington left.

"You're such a know-it-all," I tell him playfully.

He grins once more, but this time, the pain has

gripped him, and my heart burns with an agony that steals my breath.

"I love you, brother," I tell him urgently. My voice cracks on the last word, and I know I have to do something. I need to make him see he was right, and I pull out the item that makes all the pain disappear from his expression for a second.

His lashes flutter, and his chest slows its rise and fall.

No more smiles. No more blinking. He stills, which stops my own heart.

"I'll get Kat." I rush out the words before turning to the door. When I step outside, I find her sitting in a chair holding her book. She glances up as I near her and offers me a sad smile. "You need to go in there," I choke.

She nods. There's nothing more to say because I know it's the last time we'll get to speak to Ember. The last time he'll hear our voices and know how much we love him.

The moment Kat disappears into the room, I wait to hear the beep—the long, fatal sound that will alert the doctors and nurses. The door clicks and my breath is stolen. My lungs feel heavy. My heart is ripped from my chest as I close my eyes and focus on trying to ground myself.

I flop into the chair and blink. Salty tears fall from my eyes, and I allow them to cascade. There's no longer any way I can hold in the pain. It needs to be expelled. It needs to leave me because I have to focus on Kat and giving her the life both my father and brother made me promise to give her.

KATERINA

"Hey, you." I settle on the chair beside the bed. "Ash said you're pissing him off," I tease, taking Ember's hand and holding it in mine. He's cold. His skin is frigid, and I can't help but shiver. "You know, at first I thought you were both fucking around with me. I mean, I wondered how my life could turn out for the best when I'd been through the worst." I blink back the tears, swiping at my eyes before I continue, "But you changed my life. In more ways than one."

He picks up the pen lying on the swing table and scrawls out his response. *'You were always special to my father, to me, and mainly, to my brother. He is an asshole but love him anyway. He'll always need you.'*

"And I'll always need him," I affirm with a nod. It's true. After all the secrets were revealed, and our admissions were uttered, I couldn't *not* love Ash. "You did this." I smile at Ember. "I know you did. I am not sure how you managed it, but you got us together."

Ember grins then. There'll no longer be those sweet, happy smiles that light up the room. And there won't be his calming words and advice. I'm losing one of my best friends I'll ever have.

He takes the pen and scrawls on the page. Once he's done, he shoves the notebook toward me, along with the pen. He shakes his head *no* before he lowers both hands to the bed. His long lashes flutter, and he closes his eyes.

"I love you, Ember." My voice cracks, and I blink back the tears, allowing the pain to wash down my cheeks. He offers me one last blink, and the machine beside his bed beeps long and loudly.

The flat green line doesn't bump itself up anymore. All that's left is a straight line, and I fall to the floor and onto my knees before I'm scooped up and carried from the room by strong arms. I don't fight. He's gone. I've lost him. And I'll never see those green eyes again.

ASH

S HE'S DRESSED IN BLACK.
Everyone is in expensive suits, but the only thing I can focus on is the black and silver coffin in front of me. The rain that trickles from the thick gray clouds above us reminds me of the tears falling from Katerina's eyes.

All these years we believed it was our father. And the answer was there in her letter all along. My father left it for her, knowing that one day I'd find her. What I never understood was why he never told us. *Why couldn't he have just sat us down and confessed?* It's not like we were too young to understand.

"In the name of the Father, the Son, and the Holy Spirit," the pastor speaks, dragging my attention back to the present moment.

Kat's hand slips into mine. Her fingers tangle through my own. I cast a glance at her. Those big gray eyes are filled with tears that trickle over her lashes and fall down her cheeks.

A month has passed since I walked into that hotel, since I offered her ten grand to see her naked, and I never expected her to be standing beside me after learning the truth, but most of all, I never once thought I'd see this day. She's a whirlwind who both stoked my need and ignited my heart. I'll burn for her, again and again.

"... the Lord and Savior." The pastor's voice breaks through my thoughts once more, and I look over at my brother's coffin. I don't believe in religion, in God, or the saints. I don't even believe there's a higher power, but something sent Katerina to me, and Ember knew it.

He was always intuitive about life, about people who came into our lives. Even about our father losing a battle with depression after our mother died. I should've believed him the moment he told me she would be there for me.

"Thank you for standing beside me today," I tell her in a hushed whisper. I don't look at her, because I know I'll only see the pain in her gaze. We've lost so much. Our families are gone. There's no longer anyone else out there in this world for us, but each other.

"Let us pray." I tune into the pastor's deep voice again,

325

and everyone lowers their heads. "Our Father . . ."

The words filter into nothing as I focus on my brother no longer being here, on the way he would offer his advice, even when I didn't want it. Which reminds me of the one thing he wrote down, which I've reminded myself of every day since he closed his eyes for the last time.

'You're an asshole if you walk away from her now.'

"Ashton," the pastor calls to me. It's time to place the roses on the coffin. When I went to the florist and asked for black roses, she looked at me like I'd lost my mind. But I hadn't. That painting in the studio was Ember's pride and joy because I recall the moment he first showed it to me. He'd just finished it over two months ago. And this is the last thing I can do to make him happy.

I tug Kat with me, and we each grab a long-stemmed black rose. I place it on the casket and step back, allowing her to copy me. I reach into my pocket and pull out the page from the notebook Ember had in the hospital. They're the last two words he'll ever say to me, and I position them under the roses.

Drizzle wets the paper, just like my tears have done over the past week each time I've looked at it.

"You don't want to keep it?" Kat questions from beside me as she swipes her cheeks. Her nose is pink, and her cheeks are soaked.

"Perhaps I should keep it, but I think it's best that those promises go with him. I have them in my heart," I tell her, then turn and settle on one of the chairs and wait for the pastor to finish the prayers that meant nothing to me.

Kat settles beside me, and I watch the proceedings as if I'm in a trance. She reaches for my hand and grips it with a force that warms me. Her strength is an inferno, blazing through my life and warming every icy bit I've held onto for so long. I know in this moment what Ember was trying to tell me all along.

I'm not alone.

I'm not all alone.

KATERINA

THE MOMENT I STEP FOOT INSIDE THE BEDROOM, Ash offered me is a page from a notebook lying on the pillow. He said if I ever needed space, this is as far as he's willing to let me move. I haven't slept in here because my heart is with Ash.

Picking up the paper, I read it. The message Ember left before he closed his eyes.

The silence in the room is a welcome reprieve from the crowd who are gathered downstairs for the wake. I'm so tired of hearing people say, *"I'm sorry for your loss."* I know they mean well, but it's the same as the day of my parents' funeral. Nobody can make it better. No amount of words can take the pain away.

I open the note and smile as I read the script.

It's time to move on, princess. Look forward, never

backward. Love you, sweet Kat, among the broken pieces of my heart.

The tears have stopped for the time being, but I know they'll soon come again. Memories are like photographs, lingering in the mind until we give them attention. Ember is always with me, just there below the surface, reminding me of his strength.

A man who broke.

A man who gave everything to his brother.

And a man who gave me the love I so desperately needed. He gave me Ash.

His plan was perfect. Right down to the last time I looked into his eyes, he knew us. He saw right through our rigid exteriors, and he knew Ash, and I would be perfect together.

Tears threaten, but I blink them back for a moment. I want to see his words one more time before I go down to the people waiting for me in the living room.

"I thought I'd find you in here." Ash's voice comes from the doorway, startling me. When I turn around, I find him leaning on the doorjamb, still in his black suit with a matching tie and crisp white shirt.

His golden blond hair has been messily styled. His

blue eyes are wide, shimmering with love, with sadness, and with pain.

He pushes off the doorway and stalks toward me. His hands land on my hips, pulling me closer to him, and he holds me steady.

The note flutters to the bed, and my arms twine around his neck. "I've been thinking," I tell him. "I'd like to keep the studio as is." It's the space Ember entrusted to me, and it's where I find my solace.

"Ember did leave it to you in his will, so it's yours to do with as you wish."

I smile up at him, "Good. Then it's mine."

He frowns for a moment before questioning, "I thought you wanted to buy your parents' old house?"

"It's time to move forward," I tell him earnestly. It's not only because of the note Ember left me, but because this is the place I am the most myself. The girl who lost her parents isn't all gone, but I'll never be her again. Ember was right; it's time to look forward. "This is my home now. I choose to stay."

"I think I like that." Ash grins, placing a soft kiss on my lips.

Arching a brow, I ask, "You *think* you like that?"

He lifts me up in his arms and holds me like he's never

held me before. Like he loves me, like I'm his lifeline like I'm his forever.

"I love you, Katerina," Ash murmurs. "I'll always love you." When he puts me down, he meets my gaze. "I wouldn't ever want you anywhere but here," he affirms. "Let's go and get everyone to leave, then we can sit by the fire and drink whiskey."

"Sounds like a plan." I smile, taking his hand, and following him to the living room.

KATERINA

ONE MONTH.
Four weeks.

Thirty days.

I thought it would be like when my parents died. But this time is different because I have someone to share the tears, to share the pain and someone who can make me see that I'll be okay.

I've just gotten off the phone with Detective Olson who informed me that the man who had been at the store the night of the fire had been found. He wasn't anyone who knew my parents.

It really was an accident.

The man had run being fearful of what would happen if he was caught. Knowing he'd been the cause of a fire caused him to flee the scene, and he's now been reprimanded. There'll be a court case in a few months, and a jury will decide what his penalty is.

All I want is closure.

I've said goodbye to my childhood home, to my parents, and to the girl I once was. I've left the pain and anger behind, and I'm trying to focus on the future. And tonight, I hope I'm able to show Ash how much I love him.

He is on his way home from work, and I've planned a special dinner. Ember's gone, but it feels like he's still here, still watching over us. And I can't help but smile at times when I think about him leaving his studio and work to me. His wish was for me to continue in his wake.

I pour a shot of whiskey into two tumblers and set them at the head of the table. The plates are all set out, and the cutlery is shining. Candles light up the space, and the moonlight is already shining through the patio doors. The glass offers a view of the sky, making this seem almost magical.

We've been through the worst. Even though we miss him every day, I wanted to do something special for Ash tonight.

I smooth the burnt orange dress over my thighs when I settle in the chair. I sip my red wine, hoping to calm myself down, but it doesn't help.

The front door clicks and Ash saunters in looking like

he's ready to go to bed, but the moment his eyes land on the dining room table, they light up.

"Kitten." He smiles. "You've been a busy girl." He walks into room, joining me at the table.

"I wanted us to do something special tonight," I tell him. "It's time to just be. No more messages, letters, and gifts from people. I want it to be just us." I'm not sure he'll understand what I mean, but there have been too many people in the house lately.

We've had maids and butlers busying themselves in the house. Ash's colleagues have dropped by to check on him, offering expensive bottles of whiskey as gifts. Within the humdrum, we haven't had a moment to focus on us.

"I like that idea, Kitten." He grins, picking up the tumbler. He swills the amber liquid before taking a long gulp. I can't help but giggle when he winces at the burn. "God, that's good."

"I figured you'd like it." I smile before leaning forward to plant a soft kiss on his cheek. "And I have another special surprise for you later, after dinner."

"Mmm, can I have that surprise right now?" he says, the corner of his mouth kicking into a mischievous smirk.

"No, dinner first."

"You're really not fair." Ash pouts playfully, and I smile

at the happiness emanating from him. These moments of lightheartedness are rare.

Since Ember.

"What's for dinner?" Ash asks.

"There's a starter of oysters, and then there's a main—lamb roast with potatoes and brown onion gravy. There's also a choice of sides—vegetables or salad—if you're so inclined."

"You've gone all out, Kitten," he says, as the chef serves our starters.

While we eat, we talk about work, school, and what I want to do for our upcoming vacation to Europe. But even as we smile and laugh, my mind is on my idea for dessert. I've never been nervous about spending a night with Ash, but this is different. Tonight, I want to give him something I haven't before.

"Listen," he says, pushing his chair back and resting his left ankle over his right knee. "I've been thinking, and over the past couple of weeks I've had an idea which I need you to agree to."

"Oh? I don't want to move if that's—"

"This has nothing to do with the house, or anything else, Kitten," he tells me, swallowing the third shot of bourbon. His icy gaze meets mine before he reaches into the pocket of his work slacks. He pulls out a small velvet box and drops to one knee.

"Ash." His name is a gasp on my lips, while my heart thuds an excited rhythm against my ribs.

"I wanted to do this in a more romantic setting," he informs me, "but being at home is one of the most perfect places to do this. I've wanted you since the first night you blew my mind. You were everything I needed in a woman, but you also scared me."

As, he talks, the music playing in the background changes, and we're met with the music of Amber Run singing "I Found." It fits the moment perfectly, and my heart leaps into my throat when he flips the lid of the small box.

"But I'm not scared of you anymore. I haven't been for a while, but I've felt terrible for wanting to ask you this when Ember had just left us." He is so serious. I want to pull him into a hug, but I wait for him to continue. "I'm done with the pain. I want happiness, and that's you, Kitten. It's always been you. Will you do me the honor of being Mrs. Ashton Addington?"

I can't stop the smile cracking on my face. *I have a man who wants me forever.*

"Yes, yes, Ash, yes. A million times, yes."

He rises from the floor, and taking my left hand, he slips the slim white-gold ring onto my finger. The stone in the middle is a deep, dark orange, but the moment light hits it, I notice the small engraving on the inside.

"There's a rose," I murmur, running the tip of my index finger over the stone.

"Yes, it's from the painting," Ash informs me. That painting is now hanging in our bedroom above the fireplace.

"Take me to bed."

ASH

HER WORDS ARE A FLAME LICKING AT MY SKIN, and I scoop her up, dinner forgotten, as I dismiss the staff and head up the stairs to the bedroom we now share. The moment after I lay Katerina on the mattress, I'm tearing at her clothes.

I need her naked.

I want her to open for me to devour.

I ache to show her what she means to me.

My slacks and shirt are on the floor in seconds, and she stares at me with rapt attention when I'm finally naked and hard before her. Those gray eyes pierce me, holding me hostage before I drop to my knees and spread her thighs.

"Ash—"

"Shh, Kitten," I soothe her before my tongue darts out and laps at her bare pussy. Her scent and flavor are like fuel to my already raging fire, and I want to devour her. My mouth latches onto her, and I'm intoxicated.

Every inch of this woman is perfect.

The first moment I watched her pleasure herself, I was convinced she was an angel, and now I'm sure. My tongue dips into her heat, feeling her pulse around me, and my cock throbs, wanting to feel it as well.

Her thighs tremble when I dip two fingers into her, pumping them in and out. She cries out my name each time I massage the spot inside her that seems to draw pleasure right from her very fucking soul.

Her body shakes and shivers, and I don't stop my assault. This is the woman I'll spend my life with, and I'll show her every pleasure there is. My other hand dips between her ass cheeks, finding the hole that causes her to gasp.

"Not—"

"Just feel, Kitten," I coo, watching her body arch as pleasure wracks through her. I continue my taunting, needing her to enjoy every moment because the second I slide into her, my cock is going to explode.

My index finger taunts her tight ring of muscle, wanting to dip inside, but I don't. My two digits in her pussy continue to make her squirm on the bed. Her hands are in my hair, tugging and pulling, and her body shakes harder than I've ever seen.

"Ash!" Her voice echoes, bouncing off the walls, and I'm thankful I sent the staff home, or they'd have heard everything. Her body pulses, her pussy drips onto my tongue, and her arousal soaks me with sweet juices I lap up like a man starved. Because I am.

It's been too long since we've done this, and I can't help but reach for my dick and stroke it a couple of times, getting ready to take her.

I rise and nestle between her legs.

"I'm not going to last very long with your pretty little pussy squeezing my dick," I tell her as I nudge her entrance. The slick flesh is ready, and I easily slip into her body, causing her to whimper and moan.

"I just need you," she tells me. Our gazes are locked in pleasure as we move in sync. As if we're dancing in a passion that seems to have filled the room. I know I'll never love someone the way I love Kat.

Her hips rise to meet mine, and I drive into her deeper and deeper each time I move as she meets my thrusts. Her nails rake down my back, drawing a hiss from between my clenched teeth. I'm so fucking close, but I want her to come with me.

I reach between us and begin to circle her clit, slowly and methodically, until she's clawing at me and I'm certain she's drawing blood. But right now, I don't give a shit. Our bodies are slapping and slamming into each other; it's raw, emotional, and sensual.

"Please," Kat moans, her mouth dropping open when I thrust at the same time as I pinch her clit between my thumb and index finger. Her walls flutter, then tighten so much I can't hold back.

My orgasm shatters me, and a groan falls from my lips as pleasure shoots down my spine, and I fill her with my seed.

When I roll over, I'm alone in bed, and the sun is streaming through the window into my eyes, which only makes me groan in displeasure. I shove the sheets away before swinging my legs over the edge of the bed. I blink once, twice, and by the third time, I'm fully aware that I've been left alone, but there's a mug of coffee waiting for me. "Nice."

"I thought you'd say that." Kat's sweet voice comes from the doorway. She's wearing my white shirt and nothing else. Her dark nipples are visible through the material. My gaze lowers, dropping to her pussy, and I note there's no sign of panties.

"If you come into our bedroom not wearing any underwear you're getting fucked, Kitten," I tell her earnestly because my morning wood is hard and raging.

"Not this morning. I have an exam. But when I'm done, I'll come by your office." She winks playfully. "Your suit and shirt are ready, and I've picked out a tie as well."

She struts her pert little ass over to my closet and shows me the hangers. There really is an outfit waiting for me.

"What's the time?"

"It's only six, but I need to go in at seven, so I can get my seat and be ready," she tells me, before padding barefoot toward me and planting a kiss on my cheek. That's when I notice the ring glinting in the morning sunlight.

She said yes.

We made love last night.

"Are you on the pill?" My question stills her, and those pretty eyes turn glossy. That sounded terrible and not at all what I wanted it to mean. I'm such an asshole. "I mean . . . I hope you're not. I didn't mean . . ."

"You're an asshole."

"I know. I thought that was why you loved me?"

"Love you." She leans in and whispers in my face. Her warm mouth is inches from mine, and I want to steal her and keep her here all day. "And yes, I'm on the pill."

"What would you say if I told you I want you to stop taking it?" I question, hoping with all I am that she'll say she wants a family as well.

Her gaze is locked on mine, and I'm convinced she's about to tell me she doesn't want children. She straightens, shock painted on her pretty face. "What?"

"I know we haven't had this conversation yet, and I think it's time we do." I smile at her, making sure she's not angry at the way I brought it up. "I'd like to one day see a little Kat running around the hallways of our home."

"You really want this," she says. It's not a question; she's in shock. It's true. I want babies with her. "I want you. I want a family, and you'll be my wife. I guess you should be the one to carry my children," I utter playfully, but she knows I'm being an asshole.

Why change the habit of a lifetime?

"Ugh, God, Ashton, you can say things in a better way," she bites out in frustration, spinning on her heel.

But I'm faster, gripping her wrist and pulling her closer to me.

"Let me go." Her voice is strangled and husky, and I know I've gotten to her.

"I want a family with you, Kitten. You're my girl, my soon-to-be wife. Once we say our vows, we'll be practicing non-stop until you have my baby growing inside you," I promise her. And I'll keep my declaration.

"I need to get ready for school," she insists. "So that will have to wait."

"I'm not a patient man," I tease, watching her roll her eyes in frustration.

"Oh, I know that. Now can I go ace my exam, or are you determined to impregnate me right this second with twins?"

I chuckle. It's carefree and lighthearted, my first laugh like that since Ember died, and my heart lurches for a moment. I shouldn't be happy, but this is what he wanted.

"Hey," Kat says. "Whatever we have, boy or girl, we already have a name."

I nod, swallowing my emotion down. "Ember."

She nods.

My perfect girl.

My perfect woman.

I'm no longer alone.

And I silently thank my brother for giving me a

love—a forever.

EPILOGUE

KATERINA

"ASHTON!" I GLANCE UP AT HIM WHEN HE WALKS into the bedroom. "My water just broke."

His blue eyes widen. "Oh fuck," he curses, rushing around the room. Ash races for the suitcase we packed only two nights ago. "Come," he says, holding his hand toward me. I grip it tightly. The pain that shoots through me is unbearable.

"I need drugs," I bite out as he leads me to the car, which is ready and purring the moment he settles me in the back. Our driver is in the front, and the second the door closes, we're on our way to the hospital. "I need all the fucking drugs, Ashton."

"I know, Kitten," he tells me, holding me in his arms as he places soft kisses on the top of my head. But every sweet motion doesn't ease the fear that's gripping my chest.

What if something goes wrong?
What if I'm a bad mother?
What if I can't do this?

"Katerina." My name uttered in Ash's calm tone causes me to jolt out of the fear-filled thoughts, and I meet those azure eyes. "You're my beautiful girl," he tells me with the confidence I need right now. "You're going to be the perfect mother."

A contraction causes me to bite down on his shoulder. Agony shoots right through me, and I cry out when I feel another twinge. "I just need drugs." I smile through the pain.

"Soon, baby," he assures me.

And soon enough, we're at the hospital, and I'm being wheeled into the private room Ashton ensured I'd have for the birth of our baby.

I'm lying on the bed. The painkillers are slowly trickling through me, and they're starting to work. I'm calm. Ash is beside me, and in my heart, I know Ember is here too, along with my parents.

ASH

She is perfect.

They both are.

Katerina holding our little girl is the most beautiful sight I've ever seen. At six months of age, she is the spitting image of her mother. She has those wide gray eyes and that smile that makes my heart soar.

"Ember's hungry," Kat says.

I hand her the bottle I've just made and take in my wife in her tight pink tank top and black yoga pants.

She's finished her first year of university, and I've never been prouder. Watching her study, work hard, and focus has been daunting because I wasn't sure how we'd handle a new baby, a wedding, and her studies. But it's worked out.

"I miss him," I utter, causing her gray eyes to meet mine. Emotion skitters through them, and I know she understands.

Katerina nods. "I do too." She swallows. I watch her throat work, and her tears fall. They trickle down her cheeks, and I want to wipe them away. But I allow her this moment to feel it.

"Let me take her," I offer, and she accepts. Once

I'm holding little Em, Kat checks her makeup. "You look perfect."

"I just . . . I don't know. I'm nervous."

"You can do this," I tell her, and it's the truth.

When Kat came to me two months ago and said she wanted to open her own art gallery, I said yes. There wasn't a doubt in my mind that she would be the perfect person to do this.

We purchased the space, she worked night and day, and now that she's going to have a small business where she will be exhibiting both her work, as well as Ember's, it's a blessing. Things are only looking up in her career.

"This is it," she tells me with a smile so bright, I can't help but grin in response. Her hair is pinned in a messy bun, but I've never seen a woman look more beautiful than she does right now.

"Let's get changed, and we can head out," I tell her, rising with little Em.

When we reach the foyer, Mrs. Hargreaves is waiting to take over Ember duties. As a nanny, she's been the perfect person to care for our little girl when we're out for the evening. And now that Addington and Associates has grown, there have been a lot of events we're both expected to attend.

"Look after our girl," I order the older lady, who offers a loving nod and hugs Ember to her chest.

Fifteen minutes later, we're in the car, dressed in our formal attire. I lean over and kiss my wife, reveling, in her little whimpers. "Ash, behave. Not now," she admonishes me, and I can't help but grin at her trying to act as if she's in control. She's not.

I glance out of the window, watching the darkness and twinkling lights flick by, and I know I'll never be happier until I get Kat pregnant again.

But I know the reason I'm here is because of my brother. He made me see there's more to life than what I had envisioned. There is much more to life than work. My wife and my daughter are my family, and that's where my heart lies—among Kat and Ember.

I recall the two words he left me before he closed his eyes forever, and I remember them every day and night.

'*Be happy.*'

Thank you, brother.

ACKNOWLEDGMENTS

This story meant a lot to me for different reasons. I wrote some of the scenes from deeply personal parts of my life, and found myself in tears for most of them. But I needed to write it, and I needed to give Ash, Ember, and Kat their story. And what a journey it was.

Thank you to my BETA's—Carmen Jenner who offered valuable advice and notes. And to my two diamonds—Allyson, Cat—you ladies are amazing. I don't know how I could do this without you!

Anna Bishop, you truly did polish this raw, emotional story for me. Thank you! Your advice was so welcome, and I can't thank you enough for all you did.

My proofreader, Brian Joseph, thank you for your hard work, and thank you to Jo-Anne for being an amazing support. To Allyson for stepping in and giving it a second set of eyes, thank you, darling!

A huge thanks to my my Angels street team, thank

you for pimping my work EVERYWHERE. You ladies rock!!

To my adult, Caroline, thank you for everything! Thanks for keeping me in line and ensuring I don't completely lose it! You're a godsend!

My reader group, The Darklings, as always, you're the only place I know I'll find like-minded ladies and a handful of gents who will have a laugh without drama. The group has grown so much and I'm excited for the future! Thank you for being there.

To all my author colleagues, thank you for always sharing, commenting, and supporting me. I appreciate every one of you. Having a support system is important and you ladies provide that and so much more.

Readers and bloggers, from the bottom of my little black heart, THANK YOU. All you do for us authors is incredible. Reading and reviewing is demanding on your own time and you do it with a smile. Thank you so, so much. You are valued and appreciated for taking time out to show us so much love.

If you enjoyed this story, please consider leaving a review. I'd love you forever. (Even though I already do!)

ALSO BY DANI

Austin's Christmas Shortcake
Crime and Punishment (Newsletter Exclusive)
Malignus (Inferno World Novella)
Virulent (collaboration with Yolanda Olson)
Tempting Grayson (Exclusively sold on Eden Books)

SINS OF SEVEN SERIES

Kneel (Book #1)
Obey (Book #2)
Indulge (Book #3)
Ruthless (Book #4)
Bound (Book #5)
Envy (Book #6)
Vice (Book #7)

THE STOLEN SERIES

Stolen
Severed

FOUR FATHERS SERIES

Kingston

ABOUT DANI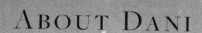

Dani is a *USA Today* bestselling author of a variety of genres, from romantic suspense to dark erotic romance and even BDSM romance. She loves to delve into the raw, emotional journeys her characters venture on, and enjoys the dark, edgy, and sensual scenes that fill the pages of her books. Dani's stories are seductive with a deviant edge with feisty heroines and dominant alphas.

Dani lives in the beautiful city of Cape Town, and is a proud member of the Romance Writer's Organization of South Africa (ROSA) and the Romance Writers of America (RWA). She has a healthy addiction to reading, TV series, music, tattoos, chocolate, and ice cream.

www.danirene.com
info@danirene.com

63128036R00220

Made in the USA
Middletown, DE
25 August 2019